FOR THE LOVE OF JENNY

FOR THE LOVE OF JENNY

Frances Mills Payne

Copyright © 1999 by Frances Mills Payne.

| Library of Congress Number: | 00-193275 |
| ISBN #: Softcover | 0-7388-5524-3 |

All rights reserved. No part of this book may be reproduced or transmitted in any form or by any means, electronic or mechanical, including photocopying, recording, or by any information storage and retrieval system, without permission in writing from the copyright owner.

This is a work of fiction. Names, characters, places and incidents either are the product of the author's imagination or are used fictitiously, and any resemblance to any actual persons, living or dead, events, or locales is entirely coincidental.

This book was printed in the United States of America.

To order additional copies of this book, contact:
Xlibris Corporation
1-888-7-XLIBRIS
www.Xlibris.com
Orders@Xlibris.com

CONTENTS

Acknowledgments 9

Chapter One 11
Chapter Two 18
Chapter Three 25
Chapter Four 32
Chapter Five 38
Chapter Six 44
Chapter Seven 50
Chapter Eight 56
Chapter Nine 62
Chapter Ten 68
Chapter Eleven 74
Chapter Twelve 80
Chapter Thirteen 85
Chapter Fourteen 90
Chapter Fifteen 96
Chapter Sixteen 102
Chapter Seventeen 108

To hospital chaplains everywhere, who minister to the sick and dying; and to the memory of loved ones: my dear niece, Anne, who liked this story; and my parents, Annie Freeman Mills and Harvey Clarence Mills, whose lives were a beacon to many.

ACKNOWLEDGMENTS

I wish to express my warm thanks to Yvonne Lehman who challenged me to write this story, to Celia Miles whose encouragement kept me on target, and to Cynthia Stewart, Ruth Burton, and Mary Lee Hester who carefully edited the manuscript and offered valuable suggestions.

CHAPTER ONE

For Jenny Carter, Friday had been slow in coming. Now standing on the tarmac, she wouldn't have to wait much longer! It had been hard to get away from her chaplain duties at Mercy hospital; but now, as she waited in the crisp December air, her green eyes sparkled with anticipation of seeing her fiance. She was proud of Grant's job as the only contact person for his company's clients, a job that required his engineering training as well as skill in public relations.

Soon the plane landed and a stream of passengers came down the steps. Finally, Grant appeared at the top of the steps, handsome in a dark business suit. His wide muscular body gave evidence of college summers as a lifeguard. With the sunlight on his cropped sandy hair, Jenny thought he looked wonderful. Her heart was beating wildly as she ran to him and threw her arms around him.

He embraced her briefly, but he was not smiling. "It's good to be back in Morristown, Jenny. Let's go," he said, taking her arm and steering her toward the parking lot. "I have only carry-ons with me."

"I'm glad you spent last weekend with your mother. She must be devastated at your dad's leaving after all these years."

"Yes, she was shocked, and I had no warning that anything was wrong. But Mom says it helps when I'm there. You know, with all this travel, I can't be with her every weekend—it's the only time I get to see you."

Jenny was too aware of that. They drove to Mario's, their favorite restaurant, and found a cozy table in the corner. After ordering Mario's special lasagna, they relaxed while they waited for service.

In the candlelight reflecting softly from the darkened red walls, Jenny realized that Grant's face revealed a tiredness, as if he had been through some great ordeal.

"Mother's going to be all right," he said, as if he were trying to convince himself. "I'm afraid she's going to be more dependent on me for awhile."

"Have you seen your dad?"

"No, but we talked on the phone. He gave no reason why he left; he insists that he has no anger."

"I guess you're fortunate that this didn't happen when you were a child. Now that you're an adult, you can deal with it."

"But it did happen when I was a boy." Grant's face tightened. "And that's what makes it so unpleasant now—we are all reliving those bad old days." On the plane flying in, he had decided not to share his deep concern with Jenny; but now, in her gentle presence, he had told her more than he had planned.

Jenny looked hard into his eyes. "Grant, we need to pray about this."

"You believe it's that simple?"

"No, but I know that God has an answer for you, and," she spoke with intensity, "God can heal memories."

"I don't have your faith, Jenny; you and I are very different in that regard."

"Then I'll pray for you."

"While you're praying, I have another decision to make. Bob Harrington has asked me to move back to Richmond. It's up to me; but, of course, he would like it."

"Would it be a promotion?"

"A step toward a promotion. He has always implied that I would be his choice for Regional Manager."

Jenny, still excited about their upcoming wedding on Valentine's Day, visualized their living in Richmond. She remembered one rambling, white brick house with a beautiful terrace in the back. She could see herself there with Grant. There would be children—maybe a little girl in a frilly dress and a little boy playing in the yard. Someday, when the children were older, she might find an opening for a chaplain at the Medical Center.

Jenny's mind flashed back to the present. Grant was thanking the waiter who was placing the hot and delicious-looking lasagna on the table. Jenny, eager for the decision that would affect them both, asked excitedly, "Do you want to move to Richmond?"

"I really don't know." Grant pressed his fork into the hot dish and looked up, "I don't know what to do with Mom, whether to move, or even whether I can be ready for our wedding in February."

Jenny, who had started to eat slowly, stopped, put her fork down, and looked intently at his face.

"It has nothing to do with you, Jenny." He made a gesture with his fork. "It's just that I feel overwhelmed."

"Grant, your mother has all her civic activities. I'm sure she will make a life for herself in time."

"She could now, but she doesn't. She seems to have given up."

"You can't change that, can you?"

"I guess not, but I feel that I have to make things come out right somehow. When I'm there with her, she seems comforted."

"Grant, I know that you will do everything you can to see her through this time. And I'll help, if I can. She'll get beyond this—and so will you."

"I hope you're right," he said, but he thought, *things will never be the same.*

Jenny glanced at her left hand, resting on the edge of the table. In the candlelight, the beautiful diamond sparked as it caught the light. Did he want out of the engagement? Clearly he was unhappy. She touched the ring and twisted it, trying to know what to do. She couldn't bring herself to take off the ring. She knew she was being selfish, but she wished Grant's concerns would all go away and that he would hold her in his arms and talk about their future together. But, as she looked at his face, she saw that it wouldn't happen tonight.

* * *

"Is that you?" Mary called from the living room as Jenny came in the front door.

"Yes, Mother." Jenny walked through the hall into the living room, where Mary was reading.

"You're home early."

"Grant was tired, so I took him home." Jenny sat down.

Mary looked at Jenny with compassion in her eyes. "What's happening with his parents?"

Jenny sighed, "Things are the same. His dad refuses to come home."

"That will be hard on Grant as an only child. Too bad there aren't some brothers and sisters to help. I was planning to invite them here the week after Christmas. We'll have to put that off until later."

"I'm afraid so." Jenny arose as if she were carrying heavy weights. "Mother, I'm tired. I think I'll go up to bed."

In her room, Jenny sat on the side of the bed and looked at her beautiful ring. Tears came to her eyes as she recalled their first dates. Grant had been the one who was so eager to get married. It had been a quick courtship. She had always promised herself to get to know someone well before becoming emotionally involved. But Grant had proposed on the first date, then on the next, and the next. Soon she realized, to her surprise, that she was totally captivated by him. Now, Grant was uncertain. Puzzled at the change in him, she could only hope for the best. The ring was still on her finger; and, with that assurance, she went to bed and fell asleep.

* * *

Grant was glad to get back to his apartment after his trip. He checked his mail, E-mail, and his answering machine before going to the kitchen to check on what food he had. Just as he opened the refrigerator door, Millie, his mother's housekeeper, phoned. "Grant, your mother is having a setback."

"What happened, Millie? Was my father there?"

"Yes, he came to get his things. I guess she got sort of riled up."

"Well, I'm coming. It will take me two hours to get there. Just keep her quiet, Millie." He glanced at his watch; it was only eleven o'clock, so he called Jenny.

"Honey, I have to go back to Richmond tonight. Mother isn't doing well."

"I'm sorry, Grant." Jenny was careful not to offer to do anything or to go with him to Richmond. She understood that they were dealing with their own history and it didn't directly involve her.

"This might just be a trick to get me back there. Her rapid heartbeat is brought on by her emotions, the doctor said; but, whether it's emotional or not, I'm sure she is suffering in one way or another. I'd like to come back here tomorrow, but I'll have to leave for the Midwest early Monday."

"Just stay there with her, Grant. I'll be OK. We're short-handed at the hospital, and I can take one of the Sunday shifts tomorrow."

"OK Jenny, that's what I'll do. I'll see you next weekend, then. I love you."

"I love you too, Grant."

* * *

As Grant drove to Richmond, he realized that he was driving too fast, and not just to make good time. He tried to calm the anger he felt at his plans being changed again, and he deliberately slowed down.

He finally pulled into his family's circular driveway at one o'clock in the morning. Millie greeted him at the door and led him into the living room. Grant, thinking his mother would be in bed, was surprised to find her there, fully dressed, and rigid in her chair.

"How are you, Mother?" he said, embracing her. "Millie said you weren't feeling well."

Norma looked up and smiled. "I'm all right. Millie just gets excited."

"Did she call the doctor?"

"No, I have my heart medicine. There's nothing else he can do."

They talked briefly; then sat in silence in the dimly lit room. Finally Norma spoke, "I don't know how I can endure this—your father has made me a laughingstock."

"No one is laughing. Please don't worry about what people will say."

Norma turned to look at Grant. "I'm glad you're here, son. I wish you would stay?"

"I'll stay till Monday; then I have to fly back to the Midwest."

'I wish you would move here. Bob Harrington would probably make a place for you here in the Regional Office."

Grant didn't tell her that Bob had already offered to bring him back to Richmond. "I don't want to move. On the weekends when I'm not traveling, I like to be in Morristown, especially with the wedding coming up. I only see Jenny on weekends as it is."

"Whatever happened to Bob Harrington's daughter?'

"Marilyn?" A feeling of disgust swept over Grant. His mother was deliberately ignoring his engagement to Jenny. He didn't want to think of Marilyn now. The last time he had seen her at Bob's house, he noticed that she had changed from the teenager he had known. Her light blonde hair fell in a long smooth hairstyle, her makeup was flawless, and she wore a very short, form-fitting dress. Beaming and sort of breathless, she introduced him to new guests and led him to her dad's important clients. Her seductive manner made him wonder if she knew he was engaged. He started to tell her about Jenny and their upcoming wedding, when Bob Harrington interrupted them. Marilyn, still smiling, moved away; and, it was then that Bob offered to transfer Grant back to Richmond.

Now his mother was saying, "Such a lovely girl—I understand that she is active in a number of charities."

Grant didn't answer. He wasn't interested in Marilyn and he wasn't sure he would take the Richmond job. If he and Jenny moved to Richmond, could he be a good husband to Jenny and, at the same time, keep his mother happy? He wasn't sure of anything. He was exhausted emotionally, and he felt that he had nothing left to offer Jenny. He remembered what Jenny had said—that God could heal his memories. He hoped that would happen, but it was hard for him to believe.

* * *

Jenny awoke to a bright Sunday and the memory of Grant's hasty trip back to Richmond the night before. When she called the Chaplain's office, her boss answered, "Tom Boyette."

"Tom, it's Jenny. Grant had to go back to Richmond this weekend, so I'm free to work today if you would like to go home."

"Great! I'm with a family now, but I'd like to leave about one o'clock."

"Fine, I'll be there."

Jenny was happy that she would have time to go to church before going to the hospital. She hurriedly dressed, and called, "Mother, I'm going to church with you."

They sat together in Mary's favorite pew, listening to the church organist playing a beautiful hymn. Jenny sat quietly and let the music wash over her in a healing balm. Again this week, as always in church, God's presence was real. All the cares of the week came to her conscious mind and answers came. All week long she had worked with patients who needed to draw on her strength—now she was being renewed for another week. *God is good*, she thought; *I know He is strengthening me for whatever I will face at the hospital this week.* Her feelings about Grant rose up in her spirit. She felt secure in Grant. She loved him so much—he must feel the same way.

CHAPTER TWO

When Jenny arrived at the hospital on Sunday afternoon, she picked up her beeper and headed for the Neurotrauma Unit, a section of Intensive Care for head injuries. She knew that there would be new cases from car and motorcycle accidents over the weekend, and the three nurses on duty would be very busy.

The unit was arranged with four cubicles on each side of the room. As Jenny approached each patient, she was aware of her training to enter an area quietly, to be a gentle presence, and to await some signal from the patients that they would like to see her. Since these patients were unconscious or too disoriented to acknowledge her presence, she paused at each bed briefly and said a prayer in a soft voice, knowing how pain is exaggerated by noise. One of the harried nurses, standing near a patient's bed, called to Jenny, "Pray for us too—we need it."

Jenny, always wary of any unbelief she might find, thought that the nurse was being flippant—until she saw the concerned look on her face. Jenny moved to the center of the room; and, slightly embarrassed to interrupt their activity, she said a prayer for all of them.

In a small room next door, the nurses had isolated Mike, a young man in a coma. Jenny often visited him. Now, with his crewcut hair and large muscular body, he appeared to be the picture of health. Yet there was no motion and barely perceptible breathing. "Mike," she said gently, "this is Jenny. I've come back to see you. I want you to know that God loves you very much and He is helping you now."

She took Mike's limp hand and began to pray aloud over him, forming her words distinctly and hoping that his injured brain could sort out the sounds and allow the words to reach his inner spirit. When she finished, she felt his light clasp of her hand in response.

Distracted by the feeling that someone was watching her, she turned to see a surprisingly handsome young man in a white uniform. He was tall with an angular build. His thick black hair fell in a wave on his forehead and framed his finely defined features and his piercing dark eyes. The name on his identification badge, Dr. Phillip J. Harmon, caught her eye just as he was introducing himself. "I'm Phil Harmon," he said, smiling. "I see you've found Mike."

"Jenny Carter." she said. "Yes, I visit him often. We just had a prayer."

Phil noticed that Jenny was wearing a chaplain's identification badge. He walked to the bed to check Mike. "Well fellow, how're you doing today?"

"He squeezed my hand just as you came in." Even though Jenny had faith in prayer, Mike's response had surprised her.

"Wonderful! That's the first response we've been able to get. Keep it up, Jenny."

They walked out into the hall together.

"Jenny, I'm glad to meet you at last. I've heard so much about you from my patients."

"Really?" Her eyes widened. What sort of stories had he heard?

"All good things—they sing your praises," he said, flashing a dazzling smile. "I'd like to hear more about your experiences with the patients," he said, looking down at her. "Could we go to the cafeteria and have a cup of coffee?"

Jenny smiled. "All right, I could use some."

Once seated in the cafeteria, Phil realized that he felt comfortable with her, and he liked to look at her. He noticed her long, thick auburn hair, which contrasted with her fair complexion and green eyes. When she smiled at him, her eyes smiled also.

As Jenny sat across from him, she was aware of sort of an electric energy about him. She had heard of Phil Harmon before—he was a resident and was well regarded. He had made an impression on the nurses. She often heard them say that he was single and very handsome; and Jenny, being aware that he was regarded as a good catch, felt shy around him. She searched for something to say. "How is your work going?"

He smiled broadly. "I've just had an interview with Dr. Chuck Carlson."

"Oh," Jenny brightened, "I think he's one of our best doctors."

"If not the best! I'm planning on going into practice with him when I finish my residency in January."

"You couldn't have found a better partner."

"True. You may know that Chuck is like you in that he uses prayer to a large extent in his practice."

"I've heard that. And, you know that I think that's important."

"He asked me about my faith, and I told him I grew up in the church. But," he shifted in his seat as if he were slightly embarrassed, "unfortunately, I don't get to go to church very often with my 100-hour week."

Jenny wanted to put him at ease. "I can understand that."

"Apparently, Chuck understands, too. He's willing to take me on, and I'm looking forward to it."

Jenny was interested to know more about this person who would be practicing with Chuck Carlson. "Chuck used to have offices in that old two-story house on the corner of Main. Is he still there?"

"Yes, but he's considering new offices. Also, he thinks we'll need another nurse and possibly a nurse practitioner or a physician's assistant. We can't do all that at once, of course, not until I get established."

"I guess it takes some time to build a practice."

"It does. But, since Chuck is very busy, I expect to take his overflow at first."

Phil pushed his coffee cup away, bent forward with his arms folded on the table, and looked directly at Jenny. "Enough about me. Now it's your turn."

"Well, I love my job as chaplain, and I'm very happily engaged to be married in February."

Phil leaned back against his seat as if he were suddenly putting space between them. *Such a beautiful young woman,* he thought. *Of course she would be engaged.* Now, for the first time, he noticed the ring she was wearing. He said, "Who's the lucky man?"

"Grant Iverson. He's a chemical engineer with a company in Richmond." Her eyes sparkled as she spoke of Grant. "He's away a lot, traveling as sort of a troubleshooter or consultant. When a manufacturer buys chemical products from his company, Grant visits the plant to give them hands-on help in using the product."

"He must be quite a fellow!"

"He is." She was always proud of Grant. "And I think your plans are exciting. You're very fortunate."

Suddenly, Phil felt a deep loneliness. "Yes," he paused and looked down into his empty cup. "I am very fortunate."

They were suddenly interrupted by Phil's beeper; and, as he rose to leave, he said, "Excuse me, Jenny. I've enjoyed our little chat."

* * *

Phil Harmon hurried to the Emergency Room where he was assigned for a two-month rotation. At thirty-four, he was glad to be finishing his long years of medical training. Today, he had lost a patient earlier in the day; then he had met a wonderful young woman, but she was engaged. As he approached the crowded emergency room, he put aside all other thoughts. He was really going to be busy.

* * *

The week went slowly for Jenny as she looked forward to seeing Grant again on the weekend. Now, finishing a Friday night shift,

Jenny drove home and finally got to bed at four o'clock in the morning. Her mother, Mary, was asleep in the next room.

The next morning, when Mary Carter arose at seven, her first thought was of Jenny's upcoming wedding. She dressed slowly and walked down the carpeted upstairs hall toward the staircase. It had been two years since Howard's death; yet, to Mary, the hall still seemed to reverberate with all the living and the wonderful times that they had enjoyed in that house, a house they had bought when Jenny was four years old.

Mary wondered how Howard would have reacted to Jenny's engagement to Grant. He probably would have liked Grant as much as she did. Yet she had a vague uneasiness about Grant's impulsive nature and the way he had rushed the courtship. She thought now of Jenny's selfless nature, which sometimes made her vulnerable. Jenny had been such a pretty, bubbly child; but now, with her hospital ministry, she often showed an unusual maturity. Hopefully, she had made the right choice in Grant.

When Jenny awoke later in the morning, she remembered with joy that this was the day Grant would return from the Midwest. She hoped his family problems had been resolved. They needed some time together to make plans.

She vividly remembered Grant's taking her to Richmond to meet his parents for the first time. The housekeeper had opened the door and led them to the Iversons in the living room. The couple impressed Jenny as the quintessence of the old first families of Virginia. The antique furniture, the art, and all the collectibles had a patina of age, as if a gray mist had settled over all. Anything bright and new would have looked garish in that room. The handsome Grant Sr. was the epitome of a genteel landowner. Norma Iverson was tall and thin, and her erect stance suggested to Jenny that she might be a good horsewoman. Norma, dressed in a soft gray chiffon dress, greeted Jenny warmly. Grant Sr. stepped forward with a bright smile and embraced her. During the evening, Jenny noticed that the Iversons rarely looked at each other. Norma Iverson, sitting erect, asked Jenny how one qualifies to be a hospital chaplain.

"I started with a Master's degree in counseling," Jenny said, "then took some special theological courses through my church's district division; and, in order to be certified, I had to complete an intensive course for chaplains at a teaching hospital."

"I thought all chaplains went to seminary," Grant Sr. said in a humble manner as if he were embarrassed to expose his ignorance.

"Many do. Many are ordained clergy, but there are now other avenues to qualify. Of course, one must have clergy recommendations for the program and must have some in-depth training in the Bible and the history of Christianity."

"Well, it's a noble calling," Norma said, throwing back her head, "but I'm relieved that you aren't a woman preacher."

"No, I don't preach," Jenny assured her. Norma, apparently, was familiar with St. Paul's admonition that women should not preach, teach, or lead in the church.

Grant's father, with a smile on his face, lounged in a soft chair with a total air of relaxation, displaying his peaceful nature.

It had been four months since that visit. Now, this Saturday morning, Jenny was still waiting for Grant to call, telling her which flight he would take. By mid-afternoon, she felt concerned. But then the phone rang.

"Jenny?" he said.

"Grant, it's good to hear from you. I can pick you up at the airport?"

"No, Jenny, I'm in Richmond. I flew directly here from St. Louis."

"Is something wrong?"

"No, just more of the same. I didn't have time to call before I took the plane."

"Are you coming back to Morristown this weekend?"

"No, I won't be able to." He hesitated, "I have some things to do here, and I'll be flying out to Oklahoma on Monday morning."

"Have you decided yet if you're going to move to Richmond?" she asked.

"Yes, I'm going to move back here." He sounded positive. "I know Bob has something planned for me."

"Well, that's great." She felt a tinge of excitement, knowing she would be moving there after the wedding.

"I called my landlord this week and gave a notice." Jenny noticed his lack of enthusiasm; in fact, he sounded sad. "I'll move my things some weekend when I'm down there."

"Aren't you happy about the move." Jenny did not understand his mood.

"Yes, I guess. I know it's the right decision."

Maybe Grant thought the timing was bad for a move. "Do you think that things will get better for your family by February?"

"It's hard to tell." His voice wavered.

Jenny thought of all the decisions they needed to make for the wedding. She had been careful not to press him; maybe it was time to find out what he wanted to do. "Grant, do you think we should postpone the wedding until a later date?"

As soon as she said it, she had uneasy thoughts. What if he changes the date? The invitations and the party dates also will have to be changed. There was a silence on the other end of the line.

Finally, he spoke, "I don't know, Jenny. I had wanted us to be together, but so much has happened—everything's changed."

Her heart sank. "Your feelings have changed?"

"No, my feelings have not changed," he said, "but circumstances have."

She didn't know what to say.

"Jenny, it hurts me to say this." His voice trailed off. "But I think we should call off the wedding."

CHAPTER THREE

On Monday, Jenny scraped the ice off of her windshield and drove to work. As she walked through the parking lot to the hospital, her hands were hurting from the windshield frost, and her whole being was hurting from Grant's rejection. Passing through the front revolving doors into the hospital, she was enveloped by a comforting blast of warm air and the thought that she was needed by patients on every floor.

Heading directly to the Intensive Care Unit, she soon found her first needed distraction—the family of a woman in critical condition. The daughter, her husband, and a small boy were in a waiting room, which was comfortably furnished with a leather couch and chairs, unlike the hard seats in the main ICU waiting room. The family sat forlornly in the leather chairs, looking as if they had been there all night. Jenny took the daughter's arm gently and led them all into the small cubicle in Intensive Care where the small, frail woman lay.

Kneeling beside her mother's bed, the daughter held her mother's hand and told her she loved her. Overcome with emotion and starting to cry, the daughter left the cubicle. Her husband tried to cheer his mother-in-law, then became ill at ease, not knowing what to say. In that awkward moment, Jenny stepped up to the woman's bedside. "Marie," she said, "remember that God loves you, and He is ever near."

"I know," the woman said in a weak voice. Jenny thought that Marie must have known the Lord, for a feeling of God's glory permeated the cubicle. Jenny had experienced this before when a devout Christian had died. She knelt by the bed and read the twenty-third Psalm. When she finished, she noticed the little boy at the foot of the bed.

"Honey, would you like to come here and speak to your grandmother?"

The boy moved slowly toward the head of the bed and said, "Hello, grandmother, I love you."

The woman strained to turn her head toward him and croaked, "I love you too, honey."

The boy cried and leaned his head against her shoulder. Jenny stood back and waited. The glory was strong now, and the grandmother slowly closed her eyes and appeared to sleep.

The family returned to the room with the leather chairs. Once the door was closed, the family cried. Jenny did not interfere. Soon they began telling stories about Marie, stories they were establishing now to use as memories. Jenny thought that this was a good time for her to leave and make her rounds. Throughout the morning, she came back to that room to spend time with them. Near noon, she came back and they were gone. She knew Marie had died.

With some sadness in her spirit, she went to the cafeteria where she was meeting her friend Evie. Evie, a single mother with two children, was a nurse on the sixth floor. She had pretty dark hair, blue eyes, and fair skin. Her small build and feminine looks belied an intense energy and competence. Today, Jenny especially needed Evie's ability to size up a situation quickly, understand its core meaning, and capsulize it in a few words. Maybe Evie could help her understand Grant.

Jenny went through the cafeteria line in a wooden way, not caring which foods she put on her tray. When she spotted Evie's table, she hurried to her. Evie called as Jenny approached, "Hi, did Grant come this weekend?"

"No, he's still in Richmond." Jenny unloaded her tray on the table.

Evie, seeing the sadness in Jenny's face, wondered what was wrong.

Jenny sat down, unfolded her napkin, and sighed. "Evie, the wedding's off."

"Oh, Jenny! What happened?" Evie leaned forward, eager to hear the answer.

Jenny shook her head. "I'm not sure. The last time Grant was here, he seemed troubled. I told you about his family troubles."

"Yes, I remember."

"Well, with Grant's brief visits, we haven't been able to sit down and finish our wedding plans. So, I gave him a chance to move the wedding till a later date. He didn't answer me directly at first. Then he said that we should cancel the wedding altogether!" Jenny brushed away a quick tear that came to her eyes.

"Oh Jenny!" Evie's said, with a surprised look on her face. "What did you say?"

"I told him I understood."

Evie heaved a big sigh. "You're the only person I know who would say that." Her mouth tightened, as if she had some score to settle.

"But I don't understand!" Jenny said. "My mind knows it's over, but my heart just can't believe it. How can anyone just turn off their emotions?" She didn't wait for an answer. "Now, I'll have to call the people who were planning bridal showers," Jenny continued, "and Evie, you'll have to cancel the one you're planning."

"Canceling the party is no problem." Evie touched Jenny's arm with an assuring pat. "I know it's no comfort, Jenny, but it's better to find out now if Grant is not totally committed."

"I know that," Jenny agreed. "And I know you have been through this when Dan left. I guess it's worse if you are married."

"Much worse," Evie said, "especially with children."

Jenny looked up and saw Phil Harmon coming directly toward them with a cup of coffee in his hand. Jenny tried to smile. When she introduced Evie and Phil, they both started laughing since they already knew each other well from their work on the orthopedic wing.

"We've met a few thousand times," Evie said. "Come join us, Phil."

As Phil took a seat, he looked at Jenny's face; and, puzzled that she did not have her usual smile, he turned to Evie to ask about some of the patients they both knew on the sixth floor. Jenny was relieved to simply listen. When Evie said that her break time was up, Phil rose as she left. He sat down again, leaned forward, and said, "I was in ICU when you brought in that woman's family."

"You were?" she asked. "I didn't see you."

"Well, I was busy with my patient in the next cubicle, and I saw you and the family pass by."

"Do you know if the lady's doctor ever came? The family wanted to talk to him."

Phil nodded, "Yes, he finally came. He probably was tied up with patients at his office, but I saw him take the family out toward the waiting room. Jenny, you did a beautiful job with that family, especially with the little boy. He will remember that all his life."

"Thank you," she said.

"I've been admiring the way you chaplains spend extra time with the patients. Most doctors would like to do that, but we have to rush off to others."

"I had to rush off too, after awhile." Jenny said. "I had people on several floors, but I kept coming back. I wish I could have been there when Marie died."

"Well, you got them ready to face the loss, and that was important." He noticed her left hand. Hoping he was not being too personal, he said, "You're not wearing your ring?"

Jenny gathered strength and tried to act as if it didn't matter. "Yes, the wedding's off."

He felt a pang of sympathy. Her face told him that it was not some casual parting. On their first meeting, he had wished she were available. But now, he discovered that his greatest wish was to see the light in her eyes again and a happy smile on her face. "I am really sorry," he said softly.

* * *

When Evie Matthews left the hospital that afternoon at three to pick up her children at day care, she was still thinking about

Jenny. Phil had looked at Jenny with great interest, as if he wanted to know more about her. Many of the single nurses would have been happy if Phil gave them a portion of that attention. Still, it was the same kind of attention that he gave his patients—listening intently to their every word and to the emotions behind the words.

When Evie entered the day care building, her three-year-old Josh looked up with a beaming face and ran to her with arms outstretched, calling "Mommy, Mommy." She embraced him and felt the gentle, sweet warmth of his little body. These evening reunions were so fulfilling; but it was painful in the mornings—he always cried when she left.

Sally, who was five, really liked the kindergarten there. She ran toward Evie, waving a crayon drawing of some human-like figures against a multi-colored background, calling "Mommy, look what I did!"

Evie swept her into her arms and kissed her. "Darling, that's beautiful."

After fastening Josh into his car seat and buckling in Sally, she drove to the market. She put Josh in the cart and told Sally to stay near her, as they went up and down the aisles and loaded the cart. Standing in a long line at the check-out counter, Evie thought of her ex-husband, Dan, and the freedom that he and his new wife Connie had. Dan had a professional salary, Connie didn't have to work, and they apparently went out to dinner often and visited with friends. Evie felt that parenting was unevenly divided, if not by nature—then by divorce.

Once home, she settled the children down with their toys and went into the kitchen to prepare dinner. Later she bathed the children, read to them, and put them to bed. Tired, she took a shower, put on a soft robe, and, at last, sat down to rest.

The phone rang. It was Dan. "Connie and I would like the children to be with us at Christmas this year. We can pick them up Christmas Eve and bring them back the day after Christmas."

All sorts of emotions filled her. Could she be apart from them on Christmas? She had looked forward to watching them open their gifts. She felt for a moment that she couldn't let them go. But sensing how much Dan wanted to be with them, she finally agreed.

"Thank you, Evie, I appreciate this. Connie will be happy too. We'll be there in the early afternoon on Christmas Eve."

Her mind searched for a way to fill the loneliness she knew she would feel without the children. She would volunteer to work on Christmas Day—the hospital would need her, and she could use the money. On Christmas Eve, she would be having dinner at Jenny's house, where she had spent so many happy times over the years. *I can deal with this,* she told herself.

* * *

The weather was cold on Christmas Eve. The roads were icy as Evie drove to Jenny's house. Jenny greeted her at the door with a big hug. The living room looked and smelled like Christmas. A fire glowed in the fireplace, and red candles, holly, and a fresh green garland decorated the mantel. Evie looked around the room and noticed the familiar, richly colored oriental rug in front of the fireplace, and, to one side, a brown leather recliner, where Jenny's father used to sit. The deep, soft green couch near the fireplace reminded her of the many times their friends had gathered there at childhood parties. On the other side of the room, a shining mahogany table covered with silver-framed photographs sat in front of a beautiful bay window, framed by sheer ruffled curtains pinned back at the sides.

Mary Carter led them into the dining room for their holiday feast. Evie felt a warm attachment to that room with its large mahogany table and its tall ladder-back chairs. With a heart full of thankfulness, she shared one of Mary's special feasts and began to feel the joy of Christmas. Words failed her when she wanted to express her appreciation. She said simply, "What a wonderful meal. It's great to be with you two at Christmas!"

Mary smiled and said, "It's wonderful to have you, Evie."

They opened presents in the living room. Mary handed a small box to Jenny. "I have always planned to give this to you, Jenny," she said. "I think this is the right time."

Mary and Evie watched as Jenny peeled away the paper. She opened the box to find her grandmother's ring, a beautiful sapphire with a circle of small diamonds. A tear came to her eye as she slid the ring on her left hand and remembered the warm security she used to feel in her grandmother's presence.

"Thank you, Mother." It was good to have family love that would not change when circumstances changed. She hugged her mother. "You are so sweet. You always know exactly what I need."

Mary, never one to dwell on sadness, said, "You deserve it, Jenny. Now, I need to go to the den to make my annual calls to the family. Evie, make yourself at home."

After she left, Evie said, "This is my first Christmas without my little ones."

"You're holding up pretty well."

"It won't be long till they're back again," Evie said. She tucked her legs under her on the couch. "Jenny, how are you holding up?"

"My mind keeps going to the Iverson's beautiful house in Richmond, all decorated for Christmas." Jenny, sitting on the couch, stared into the fire. "And Grant—I wonder how he's spending Christmas. Mrs. Iverson had invited me there for the holidays, and one of Grant's friends had planned a party for us."

Trying not to appear sad, Jenny went over to put a log on the fire.

"Jenny, you will meet someone else some day," Evie said, "someone who deserves you. Then, you'll be glad this happened."

"No." Jenny turned from the fireplace and looked at Evie. "I don't believe I could trust again." She returned to the couch. "I know it's irrational, Evie, but I don't want to risk falling in love again."

CHAPTER FOUR

When Phil Harmon entered Chuck Carlson's office in the old house, he was surprised at its homey atmosphere. The old living room with its high ceilings served as a waiting room and was filled with patients reading magazines and children on the floor with toys and coloring books.

Chuck, beaming at the sight of Phil, came out of his office with an outstretched hand to welcome him. A large man with a round face, Chuck was still handsome at forty. His blond hair receded slightly from his forehead, and there was a youthful, happy expression in his twinkling blue eyes. He led Phil into his cramped little office, a former pantry, now lined with shelves full of medical books and journals.

"Have a seat. We can start planning the move," he said, handing Phil a blueprint of the new offices and pointing out the examining rooms on each side of the building. "The ones on the left are mine," he said; "then you'll be on the other side with your office adjacent. Here in the center, between the waiting room and the examining rooms, we'll put the laboratory, the X-ray room, and the staff area with medical files and desks for taking insurance claims."

"Looks pretty impressive."

"Later we'll be getting other equipment. Chuck paused and looked at Phil. "Phil, I want you to hire your own nurse assistant."

"I have someone in mind." Phil looked up from the blueprint. "Evie Matthews, one of the hospital nurses I've worked with. I'd like to bring her over to meet you."

"I'd be happy to meet her anytime, but it's your decision. Find out what the hospital pays her and offer her ten or twenty percent more; and we could probably give her a raise after her first six months. We want good people."

Chuck's receptionist called on the phone, and he sighed as he hung up. "I'd like to talk longer but my patient is waiting. Do you have any questions?"

"Can't think of any. We've signed the legal papers, so I guess we're set."

Chuck arose and patted Phil's shoulder. "I feel very positive about our new partnership, Phil."

"And I can't wait to get on board," Phil said, as they shook hands.

Phil drove back to the hospital and went directly to find Evie on the sixth floor to offer her the job. "You'd be part of our team," he said, "but you would be my assistant. I'd really like to have you."

"Sounds wonderful, Phil," she said, "but it's a big change." She looked away and thought a moment. *The job has no night shifts. I could always be with the children at night.*

Phil urged, "You and I would start together when the new building is ready later this month."

"I'll take it," she said, smiling at Phil as if he had given her a gift.

"Great," Phil said. "I'd like to take you over to meet Chuck on Thursday."

"I can go when I get off at three."

"OK, it's settled then." Phil was relieved

On Thursday, Phil, relaxed and smiling at the wheel, drove Evie to see Chuck. "Chuck's practice is growing, and I think this job will be a good opportunity for you, Evie. I thought we could set up a system right away where you can screen the patients."

"Fine with me."

Phil turned the car onto Baker Street, and Evie suddenly remembered that Grant Iverson lived here. Looking down the street, she saw his apartment house and his red Porsche parked in front. Then she saw Grant! She nudged Phil to look. "That's Grant Iverson, Jenny's friend."

Phil turned to see a husky young blonde man in blue jeans

loading luggage and boxes into his car. *So that's the illustrious Grant*, he thought, and he felt an instant dislike.

"He's moving!" Evie said. Grant did not look up and see them as they passed his car. Evie turned around and looked back. "Isn't that something? He told Jenny he would get his things some weekend when he was in town; but why is he here on a weekday?"

"Maybe he has the day off." Phil tried to act as if he weren't too interested. "What's he like anyway?"

"I always thought Grant was nice, but I don't like the way he dumped Jenny," she said, settling back into her seat. "Now she's sour on romance. I don't think she'll let anyone get close to her again; that is, anyone other than a friend."

"A beautiful young woman like Jenny?" Phil said in surprise. "Surely someone can touch her heart."

"Maybe, when she's had more time, but right now her mind is set against it."

This was sad news to Phil. He didn't like to think of Jenny living her life without love and without marriage and children. "Such a waste," he mumbled.

"What?" Evie looked at him.

"Oh, it's nothing. Here we are." Phil said, as they pulled up in front of the sign, "CHARLES M. CARLSON, M.D."

Chuck met them in the waiting room with a broad smile on his face. His blue eyes brightened when he saw Evie. He led them into his office.

"Evie, I'm delighted that you'll be working on our team," he said, as he held a chair for her. "I think you'll like the new offices. I hired a professional firm to do the design." He handed her the blueprint. "Yours and Phil's area will be self-contained and close to the laboratory and clerical staff."

Evie looked down at the blueprint and saw the name of her ex-husband's firm and, above it in the bottom corner, "Daniel L. Matthews, Architect." Her heart skipped a beat as she looked at Dan's drawings and his masculine signature, but all she said was, "It looks ideal."

"We hope to open in late January, but you can come aboard as soon as you're free," Chuck answered.

As Evie and Phil were leaving, Chuck shook Evie's hand and smiled at her. "It's been a pleasure to meet you, Evie." *A real pleasure*, he was thinking.

After they left, Chuck sat down to do some paper work before his next appointment. He felt as if a cyclone had hit him. His mind was full of that beautiful little brunette with the blue eyes he had just met. Phil hadn't told him how attractive she was. Could this be someone that Phil was interested in? But it was, after all, their business, he decided.

Rising quickly to go to his next patient, he felt anew that deep loneliness he had had since Laura died. Losing her was like losing part of himself. Moving swiftly, he deliberately changed his thoughts to the new offices.

* * *

Back at the hospital parking lot, Evie thanked Phil, then left in her own car to pick up her children. Chuck had struck her as a very genuine, kind person, and she felt grateful for her new job.

Thinking of Grant's sudden move filled her with uneasiness. She had hoped he would stay in Morristown awhile longer. She didn't want him to just disappear from Jenny's life altogether; at least, not until Jenny had time to get over him. Should she tell Jenny? Evie hesitated to bring up Grant, since Jenny had been strangely silent about him lately. Then she picked up her children, and, seeing their delight at her arrival, she forgot everything else for the moment.

* * *

That night, Jenny was getting ready to go to the hospital for an evening shift, and Mary was reading in the living room when Evie called her. Jenny hung up the phone, and turned to Mary, "Mother,

Evie is going to work for Dr. Chuck Carlson and his new partner, Phil Harmon!"

"Wonderful."

"She is really excited. I don't know when I've seen her this happy. She'll be Dr. Harmon's nurse. You don't know him—he's just finishing his residency at the hospital."

"Is he single?"

Jenny frowned. "Yes, why?"

"Because I want Evie to meet someone nice."

"Well, they are both attractive people. They get along very well, but I don't see any sign of romance."

"You never know," Mary said.

Jenny pulled on her gloves, said goodbye, and went out into the night.

* * *

At the hospital, Jenny's beeper signaled her to the Emergency Room as soon as she arrived. Entering the ER, she found Phil Harmon and a team of residents trying to stop the bleeding of a man with stab wounds. "He's been in a barroom brawl," a nurse whispered to Jenny. "His best friend stabbed him,"

Jenny, thinking there was little she could do, stepped back out of the way of the medical team. But, at that moment, the man, drunk and raving, locked eyes with her. "Lady, ya gotta go git my brother—my buddy stabbed me but it weren't his fault—he'us drunk. My brother'll kill 'im."

Jenny stepped forward and patted his arm. "The police will protect him from your brother," she assured him. "They brought you here."

The medical team worked to clean up the man's wounds, and someone handed Phil a syringe. There were no stab wounds on the man's chest or stomach, only on his legs. While Jenny was talking, the man was looking at her with a look of fright and confusion. Phil administered the injection; and, as the man opened his mouth to answer Jenny, the shot suddenly took effect—his eyes closed and his head dropped to the side.

Jenny stepped out of the pool of blood and moved toward the door. Phil saw her leaving, her beautiful red hair falling to her shoulders. Thinking that the scene might have shaken her, he followed her into the hall. "He's going to be all right, Jenny," he said. "These are just surface wounds."

"That's good," Jenny said, looking at him calmly.

Phil, finding that she didn't need his protection or reassurance, decided to tease her. "But that man was really glad to see you."

"I know," she quipped, smiling, "but will he remember me in the morning?"

Phil flashed that smile of his; and, as Jenny walked away, she had to admit that, when Phil smiled, he was dazzling.

CHAPTER FIVE

By mid-January, Evie had left the hospital and was ready to start work in Chuck's new office. As she entered the large waiting room, she saw three heavy couches and matching chairs covered with a dull magenta woven fabric that contrasted with the carpets and pine-paneled walls. The effect was modern but rustic. Three of the walls had large, glass, floor-to-ceiling windows that brought in the rich, green forest outside. One wall had an opening for a reception desk, and Evie could see through that area to the medical files room beyond. The pine-paneled ceiling slanted upward to a skylight in the center, and gold-toned ceiling fans and glass light fixtures were mounted on the side panels below the skylight.

In Phil's wing, a small nurses' station opened onto a hall with doors to four examination rooms. Evie went to work on her checklist of supplies to be ordered, and she was unpacking some boxes when Chuck came by to see how she was doing. "It's good to have you here, Evie." He tried to sound impersonal. "Are you finding your way around?"

"Yes. Chuck, this office is a dream. You've thought of everything."

"Well, we worked closely with Dan Matthews on the planning. Say, are you any kin to Dan?"

"I'm afraid so." She looked away from Chuck's intent gaze. "Dan is—ah—my ex-husband."

"Oh, I didn't know." Chuck said. He instinctively stepped back, as if he wanted to retract his question.

"That's all right, Chuck. I should have mentioned it when you showed me the blueprints. Dan has remarried, but I still take pride in his designs. I've always thought he was gifted."

"Well, that's for sure. I outlined our needs, and he seemed to know exactly what I wanted. He developed this floor plan, and you can see how it allows an easy flow of our patients. I have to confess, I'm getting a kick out of all the newness and convenience. Especially after our old house downtown. My office was in a pantry; and, to make examination rooms, we had to partition off old bedrooms, which weren't too big to start with."

"I'm sure you enjoy this," she said, indicating the many rooms with a sweep of her hand. "You know what I especially like?" She didn't wait for Chuck to answer, but, feeling his rapt attention, nervously talked on. "Those wonderful woods and the great view of them from the waiting room. Also the way the woods surround the spacious parking lot. It's like being in the country, yet we are not far from town."

"That's why I picked this piece of land." He turned to go. "Now Evie, let me know if you need anything."

"Thanks, I will. Phil has another week at the hospital, and I hope to have our offices organized by the time he joins us."

"That's a girl!" Chuck called, as he suddenly left the room.

* * *

Two days before the office opened, Phil joined the new staff and toured the building with Chuck and Evie. He met Sarah, Chuck's secretary, and Martha, his nurse.

"We have some new clerks coming in tomorrow and Sarah will train them," Chuck said. His smile showed everyone his delight. Chuck looked at Evie, then at Phil. "What about Evie's work—she has you pretty well set up, hasn't she?"

"She sure has—everything is perfect." Phil smiled at Evie, "I don't know how to thank you, Evie."

"It was fun," she said, smiling.

Chuck, holding a bunch of files under his arm, turned serious. "Phil, I'd like to sit down with you and go over these files of patients who'll be coming to you."

"Sounds good," Phil said. As they reviewed each file, Phil realized that he had worked toward this all his life. After the conference, he worked in his new office, putting his medical books on the shelves and enjoying the smell of newly cut wood and freshly painted surfaces.

* * *

Jenny was catching up with paper work in her office, when she saw Connie Matthews's name on the hospital admissions list. Dan's wife was having knee surgery tomorrow morning.

The orthopedic wing on the sixth floor looked empty to Jenny—it always did since Evie had left to work in the new office. Entering Room 609, Jenny found Connie sitting up in bed, next to a huge bouquet of roses. Her long oval face was framed by her long brown hair. She stared at Jenny with large eyes, but she did not smile.

"Connie, I'm Jenny Carter, a chaplain here in the hospital. We've met, but you may not remember me."

"Oh, yes, I remember," Connie said. "You're Evie's friend. I met you when we picked up the children one time. Come and sit with me—I'm lonely."

Jenny took a chair near Connie's bed and asked about her surgery. "Are you in pain?

"I have medicine for it," she said, with a scowl on her face, "I'm just so tired of sitting here."

"Maybe Dan will come after work."

"Oh, he comes twice a day—he was here at lunch time. It just seems so long until he comes back at five."

Just then Dan appeared in the doorway. He moved swiftly to Connie's bedside, bent over, and kissed her. "Hello," he said. Then he saw Jenny. "Well, Jenny, it's good to see you."

"You too, Dan. You look well." And he did. Dan, medium height with a slight build, had bright red hair and blue eyes. He wore an immaculate sport shirt and crisp chino pants. Dan always looked as if he were in motion, even in repose—like a frozen frame of a movie, poised for sudden movement. He stood now with his hands in his pockets. His blue eyes beamed at Connie. "So, how's your afternoon?"

"You're here early," she said, as if he were somehow in error. "It's only four o'clock."

"I've been out in the field. Thought I'd stop by on the way back to the office. You say you get so lonely during the afternoon." He looked up. "Jenny, I understand that Evie's gone to work with Chuck Carlson."

"Yes, and she likes it."

"That's good. You know, I designed their new offices."

"No, I didn't know. I've only seen the outside of the building, but it's beautiful."

Connie looked impatient. "When are you coming back, Dan?"

"I'll be back around six tonight. Can I bring you anything?"

"Yes! I'd like a hot dog with mustard and onions. I don't like their food here."

"OK." Dan pecked her on the check; then, waving to Jenny, he left.

Connie leveled her large, deep-set eyes at Jenny. "He doesn't understand why I get lonely. He would too, if he had to sit around all day."

Jenny nodded agreement; but she was thinking about how lonely Evie had been lonely these last two years.

Connie frowned. "We were going on a cruise, but then this knee got bad and we had to cancel. You know, Dan works all the time."

Jenny arose. "Connie, I'd better go along. I'll come and check on you after your surgery tomorrow." She hesitated, then said, "Would you like a prayer?"

"I think I need one," Connie said in a petulant voice. Jenny said a short prayer before leaving; and, as she walked away from Connie's room, she remembered Dan and Evie's wedding—such a happy time, full of promise for the future. Jenny was the maid of honor, Evie was a beautiful bride, and Dan, the groom, had been so in love with Evie.

* * *

After a hectic day at the medical office, Evie Matthews felt tired and happy. Once the children were in bed, she talked to Jenny on the phone. Learning about Connie in the hospital and Dan's visits made her a little sad. She remembered her hospital stay after the divorce and how deeply she had longed to have Dan at her side.

To shake off a feeling of self-pity, she got up and started to straighten the living room—there was always plenty to do. The sad feeling would not leave, so she sat down and reached for her Bible on the table. Her eyes fell on Isaiah 54:6-8, and she read that the Lord had called Israel like a young wife forsaken and distressed in spirit. Here it is, she thought, God knows the heartbreak of women whose husbands have abandoned them. Then, she realized that she was not alone. Women through the ages had experienced this rejection. But then, as she read on, the scriptures said that God with great compassion would restore Israel; and, extending the scriptures to her own situation, she knew that God would restore her. She knew that God loved her with an overflowing love; and, comforted, she struggled again to put old things behind.

* * *

On Saturday, Connie Mathews was ready to go home. As she sat waiting for Dan to pick her up, she struggled again with an oppressive image—Evie. It had always bothered Connie that there had been a first Mrs. Matthews. She liked to rationalize that Dan's first marriage was a youthful mistake. But Dan, enamored of his children, refused to call his years with Evie a mistake.

Connie remembered how she had met Dan when she went to work for his company. She thought he was terrific, but it took her awhile to get started with him. After a long time, he left Evie and his babies to marry her, but she had never felt secure with him. Now, she tried to reassess her position. Dan had made her beneficiary of his will, and she would be taken care of in her old age. That alone showed that she was the important wife. Her mind wandered briefly to the psychiatrist who had interviewed her—what a jerk—he had said that she was narcissistic. *Well, didn't everybody love themselves?*

She heard Dan approaching and looked up as he entered. She couldn't shake the bad feeling inside about Evie—a fear that there might be some immutable law that laughed at the machinations of divorce and would reverse her position with Dan.

"How're you doing, sweetie," Dan kissed her.

She rose and put her weight on the crutches as he took her arm. "Not so good," she said, as they left the room.

CHAPTER SIX

On the first day of February, the new medical offices opened without fanfare, and Phil and Evie immediately were busy with a constant stream of patients. Evie took the patients' blood pressures and prepared them for Phil's examination.

At the end of the first week, the staff stayed late to iron out the problems on the complex telephone system. By seven o'clock that night, Chuck said, "Well, that'll do it for now. I know everyone needs to go home. Thank you for staying." Turning to Phil, he said, "Can you meet me in the hospital chapel tomorrow morning? I hope we can have a little prayer there before we start our rounds."

At seven thirty the next morning, Phil walked into the dimly lit, quiet chapel. The lighted candles glowed against the wood-paneled walls and the matching honey-colored wooden pews. In the semi-darkness, Phil could see Chuck on his knees in the pews—his large frame huddled forward and his blond, partially bald head bowed.

Phil knelt next to him as Chuck began to pray softly, saying the name of each patient. Phil, not accustomed to praying aloud, prayed silently for each patient as he heard their names. Then he heard Chuck say, "Lord, thank you for my partner Phil. Please give us discernment as we visit the patients today."

Phil was touched. He wanted somehow to reciprocate, but he found that his years of praying silently left him tongue-tied. With a sense of peace, he looked up at the beautiful stained-glass window and the light streaming in. He was going to like this prayer time. After the prayers, they walked out of the dark chapel into the bright sterile halls toward their first patient's room.

* * *

Late that afternoon, as Chuck was working at his desk after hours, he kept thinking of Evie's blue eyes. He challenged his mind with the paper work before him; but that deep longing, borne of grief and loneliness, welled up inside of him again.

Restless, he walked to the other wing, hoping Phil was still in his office. He was.

"Come in, Chuck!" Phil appeared delighted to see him.

Chuck sat down on the edge of a chair, leaned forward with his hands on his knees. "Phil, how's it going?"

"Wonderful, wonderful." Phil's broad smile showed his happiness and there was warmth in his dark brown eyes as he looked at Chuck. "I'm doing what I always wanted to do, and it's more exciting than I could have ever imagined."

"Well, you're darn good at it. I'm getting some good feedback from the patients."

Chuck was silent a moment. "And Evie, does she like the work?"

"She seems to—yes, I know she does. She's been a tremendous help to me in getting to know the patients. She has good people skills, and she's very methodical with medical records. We've always worked well together—that's why I wanted to hire her."

Chuck had to make sure that it was the only reason. "She's very attractive," he said, with a question in his eyes.

"Yes, she is." Phil looked at Chuck's face and began to understand. "Of course she is; but we've been friends for so long, I suppose I don't notice." Phil was interested only in Jenny; but he wasn't ready to tell that to anyone yet, not even to Chuck.

"I haven't been able to be attracted to anyone since Laura's death," Chuck said, looking down at his hands, "and I certainly would not want to have feelings for an employee."

"Well, Evie is a wonderful person," Phil said.

Chuck paused, then looked up at Phil. "She probably has someone special."

"I don't think so."

Chuck said nothing, but waited for more information. Phil, uncomfortable discussing Evie's private life, finally spoke, "It has something to do with her marriage vows. I believe that she still feels a bond with Dan." Phil paused and looked at Chuck with compassion.

They sat a few minutes in silence

Chuck smiled as he rose from his chair. He slapped Phil on the back and said, "Thank you, old buddy."

As he walked out the door, he turned and said, "This, too, will pass." He laughed, then left. But, as he walked down the hall, he knew that his feelings for Evie would not pass.

* * *

When Jenny awoke and saw that it was snowing outside, she remembered that this was February 14—the day she had chosen for her wedding. She arose and looked at herself in the mirror—a pretty girl with very fair skin and sad green eyes. Her long red hair glistened in the daylight from the window. People told her she was pretty—some said beautiful. She didn't think about it, except when she needed to shore up her self-esteem that had been injured by Grant's rejection. *I'm not so bad*, she confessed, looking at her image. *So where is Grant?*

While taking all the blame upon herself, her looks, and her habits, another thought broke through—that Grant might have some undeveloped part of his nature that prevented him from accepting a happy love or from keeping a commitment. To her giving spirit, his attitude was unfathomable. If he loved her once, why would he change? Then, she decided, she was reading her own constancy onto him.

Jenny, dressing to go to work, was interrupted by a phone call from Evie.

"Chuck has decided to give a party Saturday night. Phil is picking me up—it's not a date—and we want to take you."

"A party would be nice," Jenny said, thinking that work was all she had to look forward to lately. "I'd love to go."

* * *

On the night of the party, the snow had been cleared from the streets, and high muddy piles of slush lined the sidewalks. She put on a short black dress that defined the lines of her body and contrasted with her auburn hair.

Phil arrived at the door, his broad shoulders covered in a raincoat. She noticed that he was wearing a dark suit, a white shirt, and a bright blue tie. Each time she saw him, she was taken aback by his striking good looks.

"Better wear your boots," he said with that wonderful smile.

"No," she laughed. "I think I'll brave the weather in these flats."

She took his arm and they dashed in a freshly falling snow to the car. Once behind the wheel, Phil said, "I feel very lucky to have two beauties with me tonight."

They drove up the winding road to Chuck's unique house, built of native stone. One level had a core area and two extensive side wings. Inside, the living room-dining room areas were defined by the placement of furniture. The spacious room with its cathedral ceiling had an open feeling, not unlike a ski lodge.

Chuck greeted them heartily at the door. He pointed them toward the appetizers, served on a long bar that separated the kitchen from the dining area. All Chuck's guests had arrived so he could now circulate among them. He stood a moment, surveying the scene with a great sense of pride.

There was Sarah, his 28-year-old secretary who was now functioning as the office manager. She was there with her husband Greg. Always cheerful, she had been a whiz at organizing the move to the new office and training the new clerical staff.

Then he saw Martha, his dear nurse assistant of five years. Martha, a short graying woman, there with her husband Joe, had been happily married for 25 years. She was very efficient but, more important to his practice, she considered each one of Chuck's patients her special friend.

Then there was Phil, sharp and keen and always responsive, talking to the other guests. But at times, Chuck noticed, Phil would stand quietly staring at Evie's friend, Jenny.

Then, there was Evie! Evie was small, beautiful, and competent. A petite jewel!

During the dinner, which was catered and served on small round tables, Chuck's heart was full of happiness at having his office family in his home.

After the party, Phil took Evie and Jenny home. Without realizing it, he drove down Grant's street. Evie noticed Jenny looking toward Grant's apartment building.

"I wonder when Grant is coming for his things."

"Phil and I saw him one day, as we were coming back from Chuck's office." Evie said. "He was loading his car. I meant to tell you, but I'm sorry I didn't."

"Oh, well." Jenny looked resigned.

Phil drove to Jenny's house first, although he would like to have taken Evie home first so that he could be alone with Jenny. As they walked to her front door, Jenny turned to Phil with a searching look. "Did you see Grant?"

"Yes, briefly as we passed. He was packing boxes into his car."

"What did you think of him?" Jenny asked.

He couldn't tell her what he really thought of Grant. "Well, he was nice looking—blonde, husky—he was dressed in jeans. I really couldn't see his face," Phil said, but he felt that he had seen all that he wanted to see.

"You know today was to be our wedding day."

"I remember. That's why we wanted you with us tonight."

"Phil," Jenny reached out her hand, "thank you for taking me tonight. I really enjoyed Chuck and all his friends. And that house is fabulous, isn't it?"

Phil smiled that brilliant smile. "It's a great house." He kissed Jenny's hand. "I'm glad you could go." He stood there until she was safely in the house, then walked swiftly to the car, where Evie was waiting.

As he opened the car door, Evie said, "Maybe I should have told Jenny earlier that we saw Grant move."

"I wouldn't worry about it. I don't believe that Grant will give up a beautiful and compassionate woman like Jenny; so I think he'll come back for her one of these days."

"Phil, how can you say that?"

"Well, I hope he does."

"Why would you want him to come back?" Evie said, with disbelief in her voice.

"Because it may be the one thing that will make her happy."

"Phil, she can't go back to the way things were. She wouldn't trust him again. At one time, they might have had a chance, but not now."

Evie looked at Phil's face—he appeared intense about the subject. He was interested in Jenny.

"The best thing for Jenny," she said pointedly, "would be a man who is worthy of her love. I know, I told you she was against falling in love again, but I have high hopes."

Phil smiled.

CHAPTER SEVEN

Jenny was almost finished with her Sunday shift when she was called to the Emergency Room at five in the afternoon. Two policemen were talking to the desk clerk. When the clerk saw Jenny, he said, "Here's the chaplain."

The policemen turned to Jenny. "He either had a heart attack or he fell asleep at the wheel. Name's Dan Matthews," one of the policemen said. He waved his hand toward the front left examining room. "He's in there."

Jenny was stunned. "Has anyone called his wife? She's on crutches and can't drive."

"Yeah, a neighbor's bringing her in."

Jenny rushed to the room and saw Dan, unconscious and hooked up to a ventilator.

She felt a deep gnawing in her stomach as she tried to call Evie.

Evie had just brought the children home from the park and was reading the Sunday paper when she got up to answer the phone. She heard Jenny's voice, soft but urgent in its tone. "Evie, Dan is here in the ER. He's been hurt in an accident."

"How bad?" Evie asked. Her knees grew weak and she sat down.

"Pretty bad. He's on a ventilator. I'm on duty and can't leave. Can someone bring you over here?"

"Jenny, I can drive—it'll be quicker."

"Do you need Mother to stay with the children?"

"No, I'll call my neighbors—they're home."

Jenny hung up the phone, rushed back to Dan, and prayed silently for him. Then she rushed to a small conference room where she found Connie sobbing. She put her arm around Connie and sat down beside her.

* * *

When Evie got to the hospital, she didn't see Jenny anywhere; and, knowing her way around the Emergency Room, she soon found Dan lying on a table. She looked at his peaceful-looking face, then bowed her head and prayed. Touching his shoulder, Evie said softly, "I love you, Dan."

Jenny came in just at that moment and put her arm around Evie's shoulder.

Evie wiped her eyes. "Where's Connie?"

"Tom Boyette is with her now."

Dr. Ralph Neumann, the neurosurgeon, came into the room and spoke to Evie. "Are you Mrs. Matthews?"

"Yes."

"I'm sorry; we did all we could for your husband," the doctor said. "We need permission to disconnect the ventilator."

"You'll have to ask Connie Matthews." Evie waved her hand toward the door of the conference room, then buried her face in a handkerchief, crying.

As the doctor left to find the Connie, Evie and Jenny stood arm-in-arm in silence, looking at the well-defined features of Dan's face and his tousled red hair. He looked robust and appeared to be sleeping.

They finally walked to the small conference room where Dr. Neumann was speaking to Connie. "Mrs. Matthews, Dan is brain dead. He will not recover. We are keeping him alive, but the ventilator is breathing for him. We need to remove the machine, but that will be your decision."

"I don't know what to do." She stared straight ahead, then turned to Jenny. "What would you do Jenny?"

"It's your decision, Connie, take your time," Jenny said.

Then Connie turned to Evie. "What would you do?"

"It's up to you, Connie," Then, Evie spoke in a barely audible voice. "His healthy organs could give life to someone else. Dan would live on in part through them."

Connie felt as if her world had collapsed. These people wanted to help her husband finish dying—they wanted his blue eyes, his kidneys, his heart.

"I may as well donate his organs," she said at last, looking down into her lap. Then she rose. "I want to say goodbye to Dan," she announced, and Tom took her to him. Connie stood for a long time, looking at Dan. "He was so handsome! And he was kind." She touched his face. "Goodbye, Dan." She leaned over and kissed him. Then Tom led her back to the nurses' station where a clerk had the legal forms for donating organs.

"Are you comfortable signing these papers?" Tom asked.

"Yes." She blotted a tear as she signed her name.

* * *

When Evie arrived home, her children were already asleep; the neighbors had put the them to bed. She was relieved that she would not have to tell them about their father's death tonight. Memories of Dan filled her mind—their courtship, their wedding, the honeymoon, the first apartment, and the birth of the children. When Josh was born, Dan's affair began with Connie. He moved out when Josh was a year old and Sally was three. Evie was devastated, and she struggled to cover her hurt in front of the children. Soon back on her nursing job, she was able to place the children in day care and settle down to a schedule. But she always missed Dan. Now that he was dead, she felt that it had been harder for her when he was living—when he was a breathing, vital, and attractive individual, yet unavailable to her. Still, she had desperately wanted him to live!

Evie had vowed to keep her marriage vows until death. Now she was released from those vows, but she had no heart to love again. Her children had lost their father, and that was a worse loss than anything she had endured. How would she tell them?

She heard the doorbell. Jenny was coming to spend the night after taking Connie home. Opening the door, Evie asked, "How is Connie?"

"Pretty good. She took the sedative the doctor sent and was ready to go to sleep when I left." Jenny hugged Evie. "How are you?"

"I needed that time alone but it's sinking in. I'm just so hurt that the children will have no father. They are so small and they adored him. But Jenny," Evie choked, "I'm so glad that I let them go to Dan's for Christmas, since it turned out to be his last."

Jenny touched her arm. "That wasn't easy for you, but you tried to be fair. That should be a comfort to you."

"The children were asleep when I got home." Evie frowned. "I don't know how I'll tell them."

Jenny said, "Just wait until it is easier for you. I called Phil to tell him; he and Chuck want to come over if you feel like it. I told them I would ask you."

"Not tonight."

Phil called and then Chuck. Evie thanked them each, then hung up. She refused to go to bed but lay down on the living room couch. Jenny sat quietly with Evie, who talked until the early morning. "Try to sleep, Evie."

"I can't. I just want you here."

"I'm here." Jenny said.

* * *

Chuck and Phil were waiting at the Rogers Funeral Home on Tuesday when Evie and Jenny arrived early before the funeral. The four of them walked down the aisle of the large room to join Connie, who was standing before the open casket, looking at Dan. Then they all followed the funeral director who seated them in the reserved section. Evie had arranged for all of them to sit together, since Connie had no relatives or friends in town to sit with her.

Connie didn't have a church and a pastor, so she had asked the Reverend Johnny Jones to say the eulogy. Since he did not know Dan, his eulogy was somewhat disconnected. When he said a prayer, specifically praying for peace and comfort for "this poor widow, Connie," he didn't mention Dan's children. Connie had forgotten to tell the pastor about Sally and Josh. Jenny turned to look at Evie and saw her dab a tear.

At the cemetery, under a green tent protecting the guests from a sudden spring rain, Pastor Jones read a scripture and prayer. After the service, every one came forward to greet Connie. Jenny watched Evie who was standing alone nearby—looking very small and weary. The crowd thinned out, and Reverend Jones stayed with Connie, who introduced him to Jenny, Phil, and Chuck. Then she introduced Evie as Dan's former wife. A frown swept over the pastor's face as he looked at Evie. He took her aside and attempted to comfort her. "I know you'll miss him in spite of being divorced. God can comfort you, and He can forgive you."

Evie was stung by his words, but it wasn't the first time that she had been taken for a wayward woman who had walked out on a good husband. She wished that the pastor hadn't decided to minister to her just then, but she held her head up and walked with Jenny to the car. Phil and Chuck followed them to Evie's house, where Evie's neighbors had put out lots of food for visitors. Mary Carter was there with Sally and Josh, who were delighted to see all the people.

* * *

Chuck Carlson was deeply touched to see the apparent sadness in Evie's face and to look at little Sally and Josh, now without a father. He picked up Josh, who looked at Chuck, held one hand over his ear, then laid his head on Chuck's shoulder. From across the room, Evie was watching. She was grateful that Chuck, always steadfastly kind, was delighting her little boy. She said a silent prayer, "God have mercy on my fatherless children."

Soon the guests left one by one, but Chuck and Phil lingered with Jenny and Evie and Mary Carter. "Evie," Chuck said, "We hope you'll take the week off."

Evie made an effort to smile. "Thank you, Chuck—I may not need a whole week."

* * *

The next day, Peter Boling, Dan's lawyer, asked Evie to come to his office on the seventh floor of the Law Building. Peter, tall, thin, and bespeckled, a man of about sixty, welcomed Evie and showed her to a chair. "Evie, Dan talked to me at length recently about you and the children. He knew that if anything happened to him, you would miss his child support. So he made some changes in his estate to protect you."

Evie was taken aback. "I had no idea. Why didn't he mention it to me."

"Well, I told him I would take care of it; and, frankly, I believe that Dan had some guilt that he was dealing with. Anyway, he has made you the beneficiary of his largest insurance policy. That should help in supporting the children."

Peter handed her the policy.

Evie looked at the generous amount, and said, "Peter, you don't know how relieved I am. I wasn't sure how I could educate Sally and Josh. I've been trying to put aside a small amount, but I knew it would fall short." Evie paused, looked down in her lap, then looked up at Peter. "What about Connie? Doesn't she get any of the insurance money?"

"Dan has provided for her in other ways. I don't feel free to go into that, but I appreciate your concern—in fact, I think it's darn decent of you to be concerned about Connie at all."

As Evie started to leave, Peter rose and led her to the door. "I was Dan's friend for many years, and I'd like to speak to you now as his friend. One time long ago, even after he married Connie, he told me that you were the love of his life. I've wanted to tell you that for a long time—it may help now."

Evie looked down as she turned to go. "It does help, Peter. Thank you."

CHAPTER EIGHT

By the end of April, the spring flowers were out, and Jenny took advantage of the warm weather and her day off to paint the patio furniture. A forsythia bush was blooming in the yard, and jonquils and crocuses lined the garden path near the early buds of a pink azalea bush. Jenny delighted in the sound of birds chirping in the trees and the scent of newly mown grass.

Tonight, Phil Harmon was picking her up to go to dinner at Chuck's house. It would be the first time that Jenny had gone out alone with Phil.

Mary came onto the patio. "What a glorious day!" She sat down out of the way of the spray painting. "Those chairs look pretty good."

"I'm almost finished." Jenny squatted to reach the legs on the chairs. She paused and looked up. "Mother, remember that you wanted Evie to meet someone special?"

"Yes, I still want that for her."

"Well, I believe that she has. Chuck Carlson continually shows an interest in Evie. Tonight he is having a dinner. He hasn't told her, but the party is for her birthday. His wife has been dead for two years, you know."

"He doesn't have any children, does he?"

"No, and he's very fond of Sally and Josh. But we didn't think that Evie would consent to a party in her honor."

"This Dr. Harmon she works with—you said he wasn't interested in Evie. I wonder if he's interested in anyone?" Mary looked at Jenny, expecting an answer.

"I don't know," Jenny said. She meant that she did not know for certain. Sometimes, when she would look up to find Phil looking at her intently, she imagined that he had some romantic thoughts.

But, having been blind-sided once by Grant's change of heart, she didn't trust her own perceptions about romance.

"Phil is going to pick me up tonight to go over to Chuck's," she said, in a matter-of-fact tone.

Mary's face lit up. "I'll look forward to meeting him."

* * *

For some months, Chuck had wanted to ask Evie out on a date, but he usually lost his nerve. He did not want to offend her by moving too soon. He had hit on the idea of a birthday party; and, learning that Evie had an April birthday, he set up the dinner to include Phil and Jenny. He was delighted now that all three of them had accepted his invitation.

* * *

In the months following Dan's death, Evie had noticed that Chuck came by her office every day to chat. She knew that he had a reason, but she found it hard to believe that he might be interested in her. During these last months, as she had struggled with her memories of Dan, she tried to hold on to the good memories of their early marriage and to forget that Dan had turned his love to Connie. She was comforted by Peter's comment that she had been the love of Dan's life; and, when she looked at the children, she saw so much of Dan in their faces and in their gestures. She would always have that. Now, Chuck had invited her to his house for dinner, and she was looking forward to the evening.

* * *

On the night of the dinner, Jenny, who wanted to appear casual about the evening, was ready when Phil came to the door. When she introduced him to her mother, she could tell that Mary was impressed with his good looks and courtly manners.

Driving to Chuck's house, Phil was exuberant as he spoke about his new practice. "It's what I've always wanted. It seemed a long time coming, but my days are so fulfilling."

"Evie enjoys the new practice, too."

"I know, and she's a great help."

"Things will be better for her soon." Jenny was looking out the window as they approached Chuck's house. "Dan left some money to help with the children's education, and I hope she'll start dating sometime soon."

* * *

Chuck answered the door and directed them toward Evie, who was sitting serenely on a large couch in Chuck's living room. They all sat down to a beautifully presented dinner of chicken casserole, asparagus with hollandaise sauce, and a green salad. Phil passed the homemade rolls to Jenny and looked at Chuck. "You'd make someone a good wife, Chuck."

"I know," he said, not looking up from his meal. "They don't know what they're missing."

Jenny found herself enjoying the dinner, knowing her friend was about to be honored. When Chuck brought out a birthday cake with "Happy Birthday, Evie" spelled across the top, Evie thanked them with tears in her eyes.

After dinner, they moved to Chuck's patio at the back of the house. It was warm for April; and Jenny, relaxing and looking at the richly forested hill that sloped down toward the highway, noticed how well Chuck and Evie were getting along.

When Phil took Jenny home, they were both laughing. They drove into her driveway about one o'clock in the morning, and Phil walked her to the door.

"I've had a wonderful time tonight, Phil."

"So have I, Jenny." Phil reached over to peck her on the cheek, then swiftly moved to her lips and embraced her. Jenny, stiff at first, found herself relaxing. She felt as if she were falling into a deep and powerful abyss.

Saying a final good night, he unlocked her door and held it as she entered. "I'll call you, Jenny." The look in his eyes was disturbing as he said good night. When she stepped into the hall and closed the door behind her, she felt weak in the knees. She didn't understand her reaction to Phil. It was different from anything she had known. *This exhilaration surely will go away*, she thought. She climbed the steps to her room; and, as she entered, she saw the photo of Grant that she had been unwilling to remove. She decided that the photo had to go.

* * *

Phil returned to his apartment where he had left a pile of medical journals to read. There was no time for this during the day, so he tried to read as many articles as he could before going to sleep. When he finally settled down into bed, he could not sleep—even the reading had not dulled the pervasive feeling of being in love. He had been friends with Jenny for over four months, all the time thinking Grant would return. Now it looked as if Grant would be gone for good, and he was glad. Jenny was everything he had ever wanted in a wife.

* * *

No one had heard from Connie since Dan's funeral; and Jenny, going to Connie's home for a visit, found her in low spirits. "Dan left me this condominium and a small nest egg, but I'll need to go to work to pay the association dues and utilities. And I'll need money for expenses. I thought I was the beneficiary of both of his insurance policies, but he had changed his large policy to go to Evie and the children. He left me a smaller one, but I don't think it will go far."

"How do you feel about that?" Jenny watched Connie's face.

"Oh, I suppose it was fair. Dan won't be here to pay for the children's college."

Jenny said, "Do you want to stay on here?"

"Yes, I'd like to, but I may have to sell it. Either way, I'll have to go to work."

Jenny said, "Connie, don't try to deal with that now. Give yourself time to grieve."

"I never liked clerical work, and I don't know how to do anything else."

Jenny said, "It may be frightening at first, but to have a daily job and new friends at work might help you into your new life. It will take time."

Connie was not listening. "Dan was designing a house for us. We were going to buy the property next week, and he was going to do the contracting himself."

Jenny listened intently—it was all she could do.

"I would have had a nice home, a nice car, Dan's love. And, I wouldn't have to work."

"You've lost a lot, that's certain."

"Oh, I can get along a few months—probably six months, but I'll still have to get out there and find work—I just hate job hunting."

"Yes, but once you start working, you'll soon get into the rhythm of it." Jenny watched Connie's face to see the effect of her words, as she searched her mind for other appropriate things to say. It was difficult being a friend to Connie, considering her own loyalty to Evie; but Connie was a human being, and Jenny, wanting to help her, said, "If you don't have to go to work right away, maybe you could take a course in something you're interested in."

"I don't know what that would be."

"You could expand your skills; and, once you find the kind of work you like, you'll feel that each day you are making a contribution."

Connie looked down at her hands in her lap and frowned. "I don't want to make a contribution. I just want to be here and be loved by Dan. What will I do without him?"

Jenny was very tempted to say gently that Evie had learned to live without Dan and that Connie would be able to. Instead, she said a prayer with Connie and hugged her, hoping that acceptance and comfort would help. Then, seeing that she could do no more, Jenny left quietly.

CHAPTER NINE

Tom Boyette sat back in his swivel chair in the chaplain's office and eyed Jenny. "I want you to know I don't put any stock in what they said."

"Who made the report?" Jenny strained forward to hear Tom's reply. This sounded serious.

"It was Barry in Social Services. He says he is relaying only what the patient told him. Do you remember Elizabeth Gosnell?"

"Very well," Jenny said. "She is one of the very few patients who did not want prayer."

"Did you ask if she wanted prayer?"

"I did, after a time. As I remember, I asked her how she was, and then I asked her if her incision gave her any pain. She was cordial enough. I asked if she would like me to say a prayer and she said "No.""

"What did you do then?"

"Well, I changed the subject and began talking about something else."

"Did you act offended?"

"No, and I wasn't offended. I always honor the patient's wishes."

Tom nodded. He had quit rocking now; and, leaning his right cheek against the palm of his right hand, he looked intently at Jenny. "I believe you, Jenny. I've never known you to push yourself on anyone."

"So what do we do about this report?" Sitting on the edge of her chair, she leaned again toward Tom.

"I'm not sure how this works. It may go to the Patients' Advocacy Committee, but I'm sure I can stop it before that happens."

"Tom, this worries me?"

"Jenny, you'll always have some complaints. So far, you've had nothing but praise. I have a bunch of letters from patients telling me how much you helped them."

"But this is a question of a patient's rights?" Jenny frowned as her eyes searched Tom's face.

"Relax." Tom leaned back in his chair again and appeared unruffled. "I'm your supervisor. I'm sure I can clear this up. Jenny, some people aren't happy unless they are complaining or making life difficult for someone else—it goes with the territory."

"Are you telling me just to forget it?"

"Yes, just keep on doing the good job you're doing and ignore it. I'll get to the bottom of it. Now, I've got to get going—I've got a meeting in five minutes. I'll be in touch."

Jenny walked out into the hall in a daze. Unable to visit patients just then, she decided to go to the cafeteria to get a cup of coffee. She was looking absently at her shoes, when the elevator door opened. She looked up and there was Phil! He looked taller and thinner than she remembered. His features looked sharper, his dark hair looked darker, but those same expressive dark eyes were fixed on hers in a soulful look that lasted only an instant—then he broke into his wonderful smile. "Jenny, how good to see you!" He reached forward as if he wanted to pull her into the elevator. "Where are you going?"

"Hi, Phil." She felt her heart rate rise. "I'm just going for some coffee." There was an awkward pause. She was glad that there was no one else on the elevator. "Can you join me?"

"I can, but I can't stay long. I've got to get back to the office." The elevator doors opened, and they walked down the long hall to the cafeteria.

"Have a seat," he said, pulling out a chair for her. "How do you like your coffee?"

"Black." *Like my mood*, she thought, as he walked away. Still, his buoyant spirit and the memory of that special kiss the other night began to lift her spirits. Phil came back; and, smiling broadly as he put the coffee in front of her, he asked, "How are things going here at the hospital?" He sat down opposite her and studied her face.

"I just came from Tom's office—it seems I've been reported by a patient," she mumbled out loud, looking straight ahead. She spoke as if she couldn't believe it was true. Then she regretted blurting it out. Why bother Phil?

Phil wanted to know all about it; and, when she finished telling him that her boss had told her not to worry, Phil said, "Tom's right. There'll always be someone trying to thwart your good efforts, and you mustn't let it disturb you."

"I know you're right."

"Jenny." He took his spoon in his hand and held it on the table. "Jenny, you're the one whose faith has been so steady. You're an inspiration to others—and," he paused, "especially to me. Don't let fear about your job change that."

"I'll try not to."

He looked at his watch and jumped up. "I've got to go!" Then, more politely, "Can you have dinner with me on Saturday night?"

Jenny looked up at him and smiled. "I'd love to."

"I'll come by for you at seven thirty," he said and moved swiftly toward the door.

* * *

Saturday night arrived; and, this time, Jenny was not ready when Phil arrived. She was nervous; and, wanting to look just right for Phil, she changed clothes several times. Then she thought that she was taking too long and that Phil would be restless waiting for her. But, when she went downstairs, she found Phil and Mary having a lively conversation in the living room. Was she afraid that she couldn't please Phil? Nothing he had done would warrant that fear. Was she responding to Phil as if he were Grant? She made up her mind not to let her experience with Grant spoil this new and thrilling relationship she had with Phil.

Phil rose as she came into the room. They said good night to Mary and went out together into a beautiful and balmy May night.

"You look wonderful, Jenny," Phil said, as he opened the car door for her. "I thought we could go to Mario's, if you like. Is that OK?"

"Oh, yes," she said, but she was thinking, *where Grant and I always had dinner.*

They sat at one of the booths along the wall. In the candlelight reflecting from the red walls tonight, she looked at Phil as she had looked at Grant months before. This time, instead of a troubled, distracted young man, she saw Phil's radiant smile which said to everyone that he was happy, happy in his life and work, and especially happy to be here with her tonight.

Phil looked up from the menu. "What will you have, Jenny?"

"I don't know—I guess, spaghetti." Somehow, she didn't want to order the celebrated lasagna, the dish that she and Grant always loved to eat.

"And on your salad?"

"Ranch dressing, please." Jenny laid down her menu and looked at Phil. She liked the way that he took charge without being overbearing. His movements were efficient, graceful, and masculine. She tried not to stare.

Phil gave the order to the waiter, then settled back in the leather-covered booth and looked at Jenny. Again, as she had been when she first met Phil, she was ill at ease under his stare and spoke nervously, "How's Chuck?"

"Marvelous. I believe he has asked Evie for a date."

"I hope so. I haven't heard from her this week. Chuck will be very good for her."

"And she for him," Phil added.

"He loves her children." Jenny was running out of things to say.

"Adores them. He was truly meant to be a father."

"It looks good, so far, doesn't it, Phil?" She thought, *To see them together is my heartfelt prayer.*

"It does look hopeful," Phil said, "and I know that this is important to Chuck."

"Evie has needed some time after Dan's death."

"I can understand that—and she feels free from Dan at last, but her loyalty to him was commendable."

"Loyalty is one of her many strengths," Jenny said, but she could remember times when she had been impatient with Evie's loyalty to Dan.

After a silence, Phil changed the subject. "Jenny," he said, hesitantly, "I hate to bring it up on a festive evening, but how is Tom coming with the complaint?"

Jenny's face tightened. The subject did spoil the beautiful moment, in a way; yet she knew that Phil was making himself available if she needed to talk about it. Then, she realized that the work problem was very much on her mind.

"Tom and I are going to have a preliminary meeting with Paul Sherrill—he's the Chairman of the Patients' Advocacy Committee—to see if this is a legitimate complaint. Tom thinks it isn't, and he's sure we can clear it up once and for all. But I'm not so sure—Barry McMillan, the guy from Social Services who made the complaint, will be there too; and I dread talking to them."

"Just tell them what you told me—that you visited the lady and asked how she was, and only later offered to pray."

"I'll be glad when it's behind me." She felt like a whining puppy—she had faced harder things before without complaining.

"I'm sure they'll be fair," Phil said, fully convinced.

"Paul will try to be fair. But I believe that Barry will be persistent. He and I take opposite approaches to dealing with the patients. Once, when I was sitting next to him at an Awards Banquet, he said that I should use psychological methods only with the patients. He seems to think that prayer is just window dressing and that the psychological approach is all that matters. You know, I've studied all these therapy methods in graduate school."

"I guess that training helps you to understand the patient's mental condition."

"It does, and Tom and I use these methods in our counseling. But Barry doesn't understand that our main mission is to give comfort and to minister to a patient's spirit."

"Well," Phil said, "There's some cutting edge research on the benefits of prayer. We've known about the interaction of mind, body, and spirit for a long time; but now these empirical studies will make the value of prayer more acceptable to us hard-headed scientific types."

She liked the way that Phil always affirmed her heartfelt concerns. But, why was she discussing this on a date? Why was she drawing strength from him, as self-sufficient as she had been?

Phil was still talking. "Chuck bases his practice on these spiritual principles, and he is very effective with his patients. I believe that more and more patients will want a spiritual dimension in their health care."

The waiter approached and placed the succulent hot dishes in front of them.

"Thank you," Phil said, smiling at the waiter.

"Phil," Jenny said, "Could we say a prayer."

"Yes, and let me say it this time." Phil surprised himself by volunteering. He was learning to pray aloud with Chuck in their morning sessions in the hospital chapel before making rounds. At the moment, nothing was more important to him than to lift Jenny up to the Lord. There, in the relative privacy of their booth, they bowed their heads, and Phil spoke in a soft voice: "Father, we thank you for this food and for all of your blessings. We commit Jenny's work problem to you and believe you for a good outcome."

Phil's words released the tension in her spirit. "Thank you, Phil, that really helps." And she meant it with all her heart.

CHAPTER TEN

During the next week, Jenny sailed through her many duties, feeling a new zest for life. As she headed home from work at the end of the week, she realized that Phil had given her a new sense of being. He accepted her career and encouraged her independence; yet, in his presence, she was happy to lean on his strength.

As she entered her front door on Friday afternoon, Mary called to her, "Grant is in town. He called and wants to see you." Mary appeared in the hallway and looked Jenny in the eye. "Do you want to see him?"

"If he calls, just tell him I can't see him." Why did he have to come just now—just as her relationship with Phil was exciting and full of promise?

"I think you should tell him yourself," Mary said, not unkindly, and walked out of the room.

When the phone rang, Jenny was angry at the sound and the idea that Grant would come back and call her. Breathing deeply as she picked up the phone, she heard Phil's voice—not Grant's; and she was sorry that her voice had an edge in it. Phil said that he would be on call Saturday and Sunday and that they would have to put off their date. For a moment, she recalled the many canceled dates that Grant had called about, but she knew that this was different.

"That's OK, Phil," Jenny said.

"Jenny, I'm really sorry. I have to cover Chuck's patients this weekend. You know that we alternate weekends. Several of his patients are very sick, and I'll have to check on them Saturday. I may finish early, but I can't count on it. I know you are disappointed."

"I don't mind, Phil—I understand."

"But you sound angry. I guess I can't blame you."

"I'm not angry with you Phil." She would have to tell him. "It's not you—Grant's in town, and I thought this was his call. He called when I was out, and mother said that he wants me to see him. Can you imagine that?"

Phil was silent for a moment. "Do you want to see him?"

"No." She really did not want to feel that old attraction that had been covered now with negative emotions.

"I think you should see him, Jenny."

"Do you think he deserves that?"

"No, but seeing him might help you to resolve your feelings about him?"

"I've had six months to resolve them."

"I believe you. Still, I think you should see him to make certain."

"I'll think about it," she said.

* * *

On Saturday, Jenny was working in her mother's garden in old clothes and a floppy hat, when she heard a familiar hum. She turned to see Grant's red Porsche pull up along the sidewalk and stop. Feeling trapped, she rose and took off her dirty work gloves as Grant got out of the car and walked toward her. "Jenny, you are looking good. I'm glad you're home."

I wish I weren't, she thought; yet her heart was beating faster. Grant looked very healthy and manly. His face was tanned and his blonde hair looked lighter. He wore immaculate casual clothes, and walked with his usual confidence. "Hello, Grant." She reached out a hand to shake, as if he were an old friend. After all the imaginary conversations she had had with him these last months, it was hard to believe that he was here in the flesh.

She led him to the patio where they could sit in the shade. Sitting back in her chair, she took her hat off and looked at him narrowly through her sunglasses. She was careful not to smile. "How is your work going?"

"I got the big promotion that Bob had promised."

"That's great, I knew you would. Your hard work has paid off." This could have been a conversation with a near stranger.

"And," he said, expecting her to be delighted, "I don't have to travel. Oh, once and awhile—but not every week."

"And you're happier now?"

"Oh, yes, it's great—and better for my love life."

"Well, are you dating?" She wished she hadn't asked that. He would think she cared.

"I've been dating Marilyn, Bob's daughter."

"Really?" Jenny tried to sound as if it didn't concern her.

"But, after awhile, she wanted to get married."

"So you left?" As she said this, a deep and unfamiliar anger welled up inside her. Phil was right—she needed to see Grant, if only to discover this hidden anger.

Her expression must have revealed her feelings. Grant said, "You've changed."

"Sadder and wiser."

"I know I hurt you," Grant said, leaning forward; "I know I messed up." But his tone of voice and offhand manner told her that he expected to be readily forgiven. By now, Grant would know that she had cultivated a habit of forgiveness—it was part of her Christian commitment. Yet, to Jenny he resembled a small boy who knows that a doting mother will forgive any mistakes. *It's much too late for us,* she thought, *there is no way that we can find our way back to what we were.*

To rein in her emotions, Jenny reminded herself that she was a chaplain, a professional, and a Christian. So softening her voice, she said, "Well, Grant, I was very hurt and disappointed at the time; but, now, I'm sure it was for the best."

Grant leaned forward again, and his expression was more earnest. "But, Jenny, I'm back. My heart's in my hand. I've missed you terribly."

She felt as if an old emotion was about to sweep over her and to overcome her best judgment. "I missed you too, but I've had six months to get over it."

"We had something so special, Jenny." His blond hair and suntan were striking, and his earnestness was very appealing. "Let's not let it slip away."

"I'm dating someone else, Grant." At that moment, she realized how much her life had become entwined with Phil's.

"Are you engaged?"

"No."

"Then all I ask is that you let me be your friend. I'd like to make it up to you for the way I let you down."

"Don't do this, Grant!" He was being sweetly aggressive as he had been when he proposed on their first date and all the subsequent early dates. She wondered when he would suddenly change back into his other persona and run in the opposite direction.

As Grant turned the conversation to other subjects, Jenny calmed herself; and, for the first time in his presence, she felt that she could take him or leave him—the ultimate cure she had sought for her old heartache.

After a time, Grant got up from his chair and said, "I can see that you don't believe I still love you." He reached out his hand to touch hers. "But all I can ask is that you search your heart. You know how to reach me. I will come any time, night or day, if you will call." He turned quickly and walked to the car.

Jenny was glad when she saw him drive away, but she felt too disturbed to continue working in the garden—it could wait. She walked into the house and felt at loose ends. She hoped that he would not call again and complicate her life. She wanted this resolved—she didn't want to deal with these terribly mixed feelings again. Needing to talk, Jenny called Evie, who said, "Come on over, Jenny."

* * *

As Evie opened the door and embraced her, Jenny noticed that she looked different—she was smiling broadly and she looked happier. Knowing that it must have something to do with Chuck,

Jenny tried to put aside her exasperation about Grant's visit and to respond to Evie's joy. "Well, I hear you've been dating Chuck."

"Yes, we've had a wonderful time, Jenny; Chuck is such a fine man."

"I know. Tell me about it."

"Well, after the birthday dinner, he asked me out to dinner that very week. We sat in the restaurant and talked until they were ready to close. Then, when he took me home, we sat in my living room and talked some more."

"I knew you'd hit it off; things are moving fast," Jenny said, and wondered why that made her uneasy. Grant, of course. She was afraid of a courtship blitz like Grant's; but she reminded herself that Chuck was very different from Grant in every way.

"And he's been so good to me. I don't know when I've been so happy," Evie was saying. "And, best of all, he is gentle with Sally and Josh. They love him already—they rush to take turns sitting in his lap."

Jenny embraced her. "That's wonderful."

Suddenly changing to a more somber tone, Evie hesitated, then said, "But, I have to tell you—I heard that Grant was in town."

"He is. He came over this afternoon, and he had just left when I called you."

"Well, tell me. What happened?"

"Nothing. He's been promoted, he no longer has to travel, and he has been dating his boss's daughter—but doesn't want to marry her." They both laughed.

"What else is new?" Evie said, laughing. "Jenny, please stay for dinner."

Just then, the children, waking up from their naps, came to embrace Jenny; and they continued to hang onto her while Evie prepared dinner.

* * *

Jenny arrived at the hospital to work Sunday, just as Tom Boyette was leaving. Tom always moved fast and talked as he moved. Jenny wished that he would sit down and talk to her a moment about Barry's complaint.

"I talked to Paul Sherrill," Tom said, as he filed some papers in the filing cabinets, "and he has set a meeting for Monday morning for you and Barry."

"Good!" Jenny said, as she sat down. "Will you be there?"

"You bet. I wouldn't miss it." Tom put down his beeper and prepared to leave. "And you'll be glad to know that Paul thinks Barry is overreacting to what, we believe, is only a casual comment by the patient and not a real complaint. But he says we'll all sit down together and straighten out the matter. I think you can rest assured that it will be all right."

"Tom, you don't know how glad I am to hear this. It's been hard waiting to see what would happen."

"I know," he said as he went out the door. "See you at eleven tomorrow!"

CHAPTER ELEVEN

On Monday, Jenny reported to work at seven in the morning so that she could see several patients before the meeting at eleven o'clock. As the hour neared, she went to Tom Boyette's office and found him ready to rush to Intensive Care. "A lady there is dying and her family needs me. Just go ahead alone. I'm sure that Paul Sherrill will make you comfortable—it'll work out OK."

"All right," Jenny called, as Tom flew out the door. When Jenny arrived at the conference room, Barry McMillan from Social Services was already there. A large fellow, Barry's corded summer jacket was pulled apart over a gaping shirt. As Jenny noticed his relaxed position, she thought he looked as it he were at the beach enjoying the sun. He wore a half smile and looked straight ahead so that he would not have to acknowledge her arrival.

Someone Jenny did not know entered the room, a short, slightly built man with short-cropped dark hair and horn-rimmed glasses. He appeared to be very shy as he sat down behind a small table and introduced himself. "I'm Glenn Warren, a member of the Patients' Advocacy Committee. Paul is sick and asked me to take this meeting for him." He opened a file before him on the table. "Now, Jenny," he said looking at her, "I understand that you have offended the patient, Elizabeth Gosnell, who considers prayer inappropriate. Is that correct?"

"Not exactly. She didn't appear offended when I visited her. And she may have said something later as a casual comment, but I don't believe that it was a complaint." She realized that she shouldn't have said that, because challenging this insecure man would cause him to really press her.

"Well, it's been filed as a complaint." Glenn sat back in his chair in an officious manner. Clasping his hands together on the edge of the desk and looking very serious, he continued, "What we're dealing with here is a possible infraction of Mrs. Gosnell's rights. You know, Miss Carter, we must be very careful to honor the religious beliefs of our patients and even the lack thereof."

"I do that, faithfully." She tried to read his face.

"Well, it appears that you wanted to pray and she didn't. You cannot put your own desires onto the patient." Glenn gave a conspiratorial glance to Barry.

"I'm sorry if the case has been reported that way. I chatted with Mrs. Gosnell first, then offered prayer. When she refused, I turned the conversation to other topics. We chatted quite awhile, and she seemed pleasant enough as I left."

Glenn looked at Barry but his voice was soft and gentle, "Miss Carter's story differs from the report."

Barry, energizing the muscles in his heavy body to move, sat up. "Maybe she didn't actually pray, and maybe she changed the subject after the patient declined prayer," Barry, said, gesturing with his hands, "but, I believe that the patient felt pressured to pray."

"To be sure," Glenn said, nodding at Barry as if he agreed, and then turned to Jenny, waiting for her rebuttal.

"The chaplain's job is not to impose religion on the patients, but to comfort them," Jenny replied.

Barry, in his lounging position, moved enough to say, "But you shouldn't pressure the patients."

"And I don't pressure them." She looked sharply at Barry.

Warren squirmed in his seat and leafed through the file. He appeared uncomfortable with Jenny's denial of Barry's accusation. Thinking that Glenn believed her, Jenny continued, "Most of the patients believe in, at least, a higher power, and very few are offended at the mention of prayer. But if they are, I back off quickly."

Barry objected, "These jarring intrusions into the sick room do the patient more harm than good."

Glenn again nodded assent to Barry as if the comment pleased him, and, turning to Jenny, said, "It's still a question of patients' rights." It was clear to Jenny that Glenn Warren's mind was made up; he and Barry had already agreed, and they weren't even subtle about it. The hearing continued another fifteen minutes and Jenny defended herself as best she could. To Jenny, the whole scene was like a bad dream.

Warren made some notes in his file, then looked up at Jenny. "I will confirm Barry's report of the infraction of Mrs. Gosnell's rights and refer the matter to the Patients' Advocacy Committee."

"There was no infraction in this case," Jenny objected.

"I'm sorry, Miss Carter, the subject is closed. As I said, we will refer the matter to the full committee." Glancing toward Barry, whose face revealed his satisfaction, Glenn closed the file and put his pen in his pocket.

Jenny sat very still. Glenn arose to leave the room; and, as Barry joined him, they walked out together.

* * *

Jenny was glad to get back to the quiet of the empty chaplain's office. She occupied herself with paper work while waiting for Tom to return from Intensive Care.

The door opened, and Tom came in with a bluster, "How did it go?"

"Paul Sherrill was sick," Jenny said, "so Glenn Warren, a member of the committee, presided. Barry McMillan and I were the only other people there."

Tom frowned. "I just learned about Paul—the doctor has ordered him to stay at home a month for a complete rest."

"The meeting lasted only fifteen minutes. I denied putting pressure on the patient to pray, but Glenn is referring the complaint to the full Patients' Advocacy Committee."

"No!" Tom exploded. "What a cockeyed turn of events. There isn't any case to start with." Tom plopped down into a chair, needing a kinetic expression of his frustration. Jenny knew that Tom's

exquisite sense of fairness and deep compassion were often accompanied by sharp movements that displayed his impatient nature.
"I should have been there," he said in disgust.

Jenny, dejected, said nothing.

Tom got up in a resolute manner. "I underestimated Barry's determination to push this." He looked straight ahead as if he were talking to himself. "Then, of course, I was counting on Paul to squelch the ridiculous accusation. I'll just tell the committee, if I have to, that this is not a real patient complaint—let alone an infraction of the patient's rights. It's just Barry's fix on the matter." Then, Tom, seeing the expression on Jenny's face, said, "Why don't you go home, Jenny. Now that I'm here, I'd just as soon work the rest of the day."

"Thank you, Tom." Jenny cleared her desk quickly and left. As she drove home, she felt relieved to get away from the hospital for awhile. She decided not to tell Mary about the hearing.

* * *

Mary greeted her at the door. "Grant called and left his number."

Jenny was surprised. "It's Monday. He should be at work."

"He has a desk job now, hasn't he?" Mary liked to point out details.

"Yes, but it's not like him to interrupt his day with a personal call. I wish he wouldn't."

"Did you resolve anything Saturday?"

"I tried to let him know that it was over. Says he wants to be friends now—after disappearing from my life for six months." Jenny plopped down exhausted in a chair in the living room.

"Are you going to call him back?"

"No."

"I guess he finally realizes what he has lost." Mary said, sitting down on the couch. "Jenny, I believe that Grant has been more concerned with what he wants than on making you happy."

"That's for sure. He said I could call him at any time; and, of course, I don't plan to." She could remember when she would have been happy with a Monday morning call. Now that he has time for courtship, it didn't matter anymore.

Mary was speaking; and, as usual, to the point. "You are a giver and he is a taker. If you do choose to go back with him, you'll need to realize that. Now Phil strikes me as someone who is totally dedicated to serving the other person. I can't picture his putting his own needs first."

"That's true. He is just the opposite of Grant in that way."

Mary arose; and, as she started toward the kitchen, she called back. "It looks as it you'll have Grant in the picture for awhile."

"That's exactly what I do not want." she said, emphasizing the 'not'. But, did she really want to get rid of him, or was she rejecting him to get even?

* * *

When Phil called that night, Jenny realized how much she had missed him over the weekend. "How was your weekend, Phil?"

"Pretty good. I spent Saturday night in the Emergency Room with one of Chuck's patients. I got some sleep Sunday after I finished the morning rounds, but I had to go back last night for one of my patients." Phil said. "But tell me—how did your hearing go today?"

"Not too well. Paul Sherrill wasn't there, and Tom was called away; so Glenn Warren presided. He's a member of Paul's committee, but he wasn't very objective. And, of course, Barry McMillan was there, still in his private battle against prayer."

"So what did they decide?"

"Glenn is going to refer the so-called complaint to the full committee."

Phil was disappointed. "Well, Jenny, I'm sure they will dismiss it." Yet, he felt that it was the beginning of an involved process.

"Tom says that he'll explain it to the committee, if necessary; so I'm trying not to worry."

"That's right, Jenny," Phil said softening his voice to a tender tone. "You know you are doing God's work. Keep up that beautiful faith of yours."

CHAPTER TWELVE

The next morning, Phil went to the hospital chapel. As he knelt in the darkened room, he knew that the complaint against Jenny was bogus; but he also knew it could affect her job. He wanted to make Jenny's problem go away; and, in his helplessness, he began to pray for the situation. At first his prayers felt hollow, until he tried again in earnestness; then his prayers made a mysterious shift from his head to the center of his being. Now in deep prayer and praise that God had heard his prayer, he became aware that Jenny's work problem was minor compared to the prayer that was buried in his heart—his need for Jenny. He had trouble asking God specifically to turn Jenny's heart to him. Trying to put her good above his needs, he asked that God's will be done in her life and that she be given the partner who was best for her.

As he finished his prayer, he heard Chuck come in. He could see Chuck's smile even in the darkened chapel. Chuck, who was a naturally pleasant fellow, hadn't stopped smiling since he had started dating Evie. Phil smiled, too—it was impossible not to in Chuck's glowing presence. The two bowed together and prayed for their patients one by one.

* * *

On Saturday morning, Jenny dropped by to see what Evie had to show her. When Evie opened the door, Jenny said, "It must be something special—I've never seen you glow like this."

Evie held out her left hand.

"What a beautiful diamond," Jenny exclaimed and hugged Evie. "When did this happen?"

Evie sat down on the couch and looked very demure, "Last night."

"And when is the wedding?" Jenny sat down close beside her.

"Saturday, June 30." Evie turned to Jenny smiling, "We want to have the wedding in Chuck's garden."

"Oh Evie."

"You'll be my maid of honor—for the second time, but this time will be the last; and Chuck is asking Phil to be his best man."

"Great."

Evie led Jenny into her bedroom and held up a pale pink, silk dress with a low round neckline, very small waist, and a flowing full skirt. "Chuck has been talking marriage for some time; he was just waiting for me to decide. So when I saw this dress, I decided it was perfect. But he gave me the ring just last night, and it's official now."

Jenny teased, "I like your style, gal—buy the wedding dress before the ring."

"But I knew we were getting married. And Jenny, the bridal shop had a deeper pink dress in your size. Would you be willing to try it on; I asked them to hold it for you?"

"Great! I'll go and try it on."

Evie smoothed the dress with her hand and looked at Jenny. "Oh, Jenny, I didn't think I would ever feel this way again."

"God is good," Jenny said. "You've had a lot of sadness, but He is really blessing you now."

They sat down on the side of the bed and spent the rest of the day planning the wedding.

* * *

On Sunday night, Jenny was on duty when Tom Boyette was called in to attend the death of a patient he had worked with. Tom and Jenny did the rounds together, dividing the beeper emergency interruptions between them. By two o'clock in the morning, they finished their rounds and started back to the office together. Tom stopped to check on a patient in Intensive Care, while Jenny waited for him in the family waiting room. She was taken aback at the discomfort of the family members trying to sleep in the attached wooden theater seats with hard arms. The sleepers could not stretch out, and some had slung a leg over the arm of one chair and were sleeping with their heads hanging over the attached chair on the opposite side. Several people were stretched out on the floor.

When Tom rejoined Jenny, she complained, "Tom, look at these distorted bodies trying to sleep. They won't be allowed into Intensive Care to visit their families for another hour, so you know they want to sleep at this hour of the morning. Why can't they have comfortable seats for their long hours of waiting?"

"These hard seats were installed for a reason," Tom said, "to discourage the families from staying the night."

"Well, it's not working—they are staying anyway."

"And I don't blame them." By now, they had reached their offices, and Tom unlocked the door. "When I first came to work here, it shocked me to see their discomfort, as if their anxiety weren't enough. I asked why and one of the administrators said, 'They need to go home. We don't want them to stay all night.' It really made me mad. I left the room mumbling, 'I'll bet you'd be there all night if it were your mother or grandmother or maybe your little child—you'd want to know the minute their condition changed.' He didn't hear my reply, and it's just as well. The administrators look at it as a business decision."

Jenny and Tom made notes for follow-up visits and prepared to leave. "There's no use to put it in the suggestion box, then?" Jenny asked.

Tom turned out the lights and locked the door as they left. "You can try, but I think it's a lost cause."

* * *

When Evie arrived at the medical office Monday morning wearing Chuck's large diamond ring, Phil was delighted. "Evie, how'd you do it?" he kidded.

"Don't know," she smiled, "guess it's my sparkling personality." Then her expression changed to a soft seriousness. "Phil, I am so fortunate. You know what a great guy Chuck is. He loves Sally and Josh and they adore him," she looked down as if she were shy about expressing her emotions in the office, "and I do, too."

"I couldn't be happier for you both," Phil said, embracing her.

By late afternoon Monday, everyone in the office knew about the engagement. All day, Phil had tried to get a chance to call Chuck or to see him; but Chuck had been called to the hospital—to the same patient that Phil attended most of Saturday night. Phil took some of Chuck's patients; but, when Chuck returned, his waiting room was still full. Finally, at the end of the day, Phil found Chuck working at his desk. Dashing into the room, Phil held out his hand, "Chuck! Congratulations! You did it. I'm so happy for you and Evie."

Chuck jumped up to accept Phil's handshake, and smiling broadly, said, "Thanks, Phil. I am the happiest man in the world."

"I can see." Phil laughed and embraced Chuck. Patting him on the back, Phil said, "Evie will make you a wonderful wife—you both deserve much happiness."

Chuck slapped Phil on the back and said, "I expect you to be next."

"I don't know if there is any hope for this old bachelor," Phil said, smiling. But he knew that he had hope.

"I'm putting my money on you."

"Nothing's impossible," Phil replied and sat down.

Chuck returned to his swivel chair and resting his elbows on the arms, clasped his hands. "Phil, Evie says that your parents are coming soon."

"Yes, about the time of the wedding, in fact."

"Well, they're invited, of course; but I'd like them to stay at my house—your apartment is too small."

"That's OK, I have reservations for them at one of the better motels."

"Nonsense, you know I don't have any near relatives to come to the wedding. I want them there at the house—so, it's settled."

"If you insist. I'm sure that nothing would please them more than to be considered your family for the occasion. You know, this new happiness of yours is spilling out over all of us!" Phil grinned broadly.

Chuck's face grew serious. "Phil, I didn't think I could find anyone again after losing Laura. I loved her very much, and I've been very lonely. But I fell in love with Evie the first time I saw her."

"I know," Phil said soberly. Chuck was a true friend, and Phil's heart was full of thankfulness.

CHAPTER THIRTEEN

That night, after a day of excitement at his office, Phil called Jenny. "Jenny, I guess you know it's official—Chuck and Evie are engaged."

Jenny's heart warmed at his voice. "I know. Evie showed me her ring this weekend—Chuck gave it to her Friday night. And, you and I are to be attendants."

"I'm looking forward to it. My parents are coming here for a visit about that time, and Chuck insists that they stay at his house."

"Isn't that like Chuck?"

"Yes—I haven't seen them for a year. It's a pretty long trip from Chicago, and Dad is so involved in his research that he lets his vacation time pile up. They had promised to come when I finished my residency program."

"Now they can really say, 'My son, the doctor,'" Jenny said, laughing.

"And they do say it—I want you to meet them."

"Of course, I'll look forward."

"Honey, I'm at the hospital, and I have to go."

* * *

When Saturday came, Jenny went over to help Evie with a yard sale. They sat out in the sunshine, drinking lemonade, and talking between buyers. Evie said, "Chuck has put his and Laura's bedroom furniture in storage, and we have picked out new furniture for what will be our bedroom."

"Chuck is always considerate to a fault," Jenny said.

"Exactly," Evie smiled. "We are going to move the children's old furniture and toys into the room next to ours. Chuck has already cleared out that room. That will give them an easy transition to the new house. When Sally and Josh are a little older, we'll fix a room for each of them."

Jenny was happy to see Evie full of plans. "It's an ideal home for a family—four bedrooms and three baths."

"It's amazing how Chuck and I agree," Evie said with a puzzled look on her face.

"It's not so amazing," Jenny said. "The man is crazy about you."

"And I love him, too. It's not one-sided."

"Of course you do," Jenny reassured her, "but the neat thing is that you both want to give pleasure to the other. Knowing you both, I'm not at all surprised that you agree."

Jenny knew that it was out of character for Evie to repeat herself; she usually had an economical and precise summary of events around her, so Jenny was amused when Evie kept saying, "I'm just so happy."

"I'd never guess." Jenny laughed.

* * *

At the hospital, Jenny tried not to let the problem with Barry discourage her. But, as she visited with patients, she felt disenfranchised. She had always been successful in everything she tried. She had been told that she was sensitive to others and had a highly developed empathy for sick people. It had served her well as a chaplain; but, now, as she talked to persons lying on their beds, dealing with upcoming surgery or constant pain, she tried to enter into their sufferings more deeply than ever before. In order to do that, she had to put out of her mind the possibility of being fired and to concentrate intensely on what that patient needed at that moment. She sent up little quiet prayers that God would give her the right words at the right time to minister to the sometimes hidden needs of the patients.

But what would she do if this so-called complaint got out-of-hand? She remembered how God had called her after a year of studying Jesus' parables of healing in a church Bible study. After the training, the study group was commissioned before the altar on Sunday morning and made a commitment to serve the sick. To Jenny's surprise, everyone in the group voted to continue the study, rather than to reach out to the church's sick people. However, Jenny felt that God did not want her in another comfortable year of study. He was calling her to minister to sick and lonely people, to alleviate their loneliness, and to give them comfort.

About that time, she was able to enter the chaplain training program in a hospital some miles away. She fulfilled all the course and hospital internship requirements and was certified by the State. Once on duty as a chaplain, she felt in the very center of God's will. Tom had said that her reputation had spread over the hospital, and he gave her great freedom in how she ministered to the patients. Would the comment of Elizabeth Gosnell, however slight or serious, jeopardize this wonderful world of service that God had given her?

She mustn't let that happen. Phil had said to hold her faith; and she must believe that, if God could call her, open the door for training, and give her initial success, He would not let man or the devil defeat her.

That settled, her heart filled with gratitude and praise for all that God had led her through. She remembered her first contact with heart patients—the way the men, especially, would open up to her when they were alone in the late night hours before the next day's surgery. The role surprised her—they looked to her as mother, sister, and confessor.

She remembered her first brain surgeries, and how shy she felt about approaching anyone in the unenviable position of having their skulls opened and the very locus of their thoughts invaded. But soon brain surgeries, too, were familiar.

As she recalled, it was a long time before she encountered any amputees, but she soon had many of them. She learned to console them before the surgery; and, after the surgery, she learned to look them in the eye and ignore the stump under the cover and the flat place in the bedding where a leg should have been. Her first such patient wanted to show Jenny her operation. Reluctantly she agreed, and the lady pulled out a short stump of a leg with a neat skin graft covering the tip. It really wasn't so hard to look at. Jenny once had asked Evie why so many patients wanted her to look at their incisions—by then, she had seen staples and stitches in all manner of designs. Evie seemed to think it was therapeutic for the patients to show their healed incisions. Whether or not Evie was right, Jenny knew that the patients wanted her to connect to their operations.

She thought of all the deaths she had attended—she valued most those times when she was the only person to stand with a patient as he died—patients who had no loved one to hover over him. She worked hard on those occasions to be a comforting presence and to make the patient's passage easier.

Yes, it had been a good three years, and she had learned a lot.

* * *

When Jenny returned home that day, she had another call from Grant.

"You didn't return my call," he admonished.

"No, I was busy."

"Well, Jenny, I see that I can't wait for you to call, so I'll have to do the calling."

"Maybe you shouldn't, Grant?"

"You're not engaged yet, are you?"

"No, and besides, you know that engagements don't always mean one is getting married." She regretted the sarcasm in her voice. A root of bitterness was still in her spirit. It would be easier to forgive Grant if she didn't have to deal with him. There was always a hint of the old attraction, but it was always mitigated by sad thoughts. His assurance that he would prevail threatened her peace, so she concluded the conversation as soon as she could.

"Mother," she said, as Mary came into the room. "I really wish that Grant and I could part friends, and that he would quit calling."

Mary looked at her and said, "Maybe Grant enjoys the game of winning you, but can't deal with love once he has won it. I guess he'll keep trying."

"I'd like to find a way to get a closure on this without being as heartless as he was when he broke the engagement."

"Well, he can't do you too much harm while he's there in Richmond."

"I don't know—it keeps me unsettled."

"Jenny, you must pray about this. Try to discern what God would have you do. You were not the one to break the commitment, so you have no obligation, as I see it."

Jenny knew that Mary was right. Was she talking to Grant to fulfill that old longing she had felt these last six months. Was she flattered by his attention? No, in spite of an anger that rose up in her when he called, she liked knowing how he was getting along. She hoped that meant that she was moving to the friendship stage, where she could care about him without a heavy emotional connection.

CHAPTER FOURTEEN

Jenny was going to dinner tonight with Phil and his parents, who had just arrived. She inspected herself carefully in front of the mirror; and, satisfied that the white sleeveless dress looked good, she took a small white bag and headed to the living room to wait. Mary was there, reading a magazine. "You look lovely, Jenny. That dress is so cool and summery."

"It's not too dressy?"

"No, it's simple—it really fits you well, and those sandals are pretty with it."

The doorbell rang, and Jenny dashed to the door to greet Phil and his parents.

"Hello, Jenny," Phil said, smiling. "This is my mother, Grace Harmon and my father, Charles Harmon."

"Come in," Jenny smiled broadly at them. "I'm so glad to meet you at last." They followed her into the living room. "Mother, this is Dr. and Mrs. Harmon, Phil's parents—my mother, Mary Carter."

As Mary rose and extended her hand to greet them, Phil stood behind his parents. "I've spoken so often of Jenny and Mary—they wanted to meet you both."

When all were seated, Dr. Charles Harmon leaned back as if he were very comfortable and, with a large smile, looked at Phil. "We've been wanting to visit Phil ever since he finished his residency. It's good to be here at last."

"I'm sure you're very proud of him," Mary said.

Charles nodded, and Grace smiled and said, "Very!"

"How was your flight?" Jenny asked.

"Very comfortable," Charles answered. "In fact, Phil dropped off our luggage at Chuck's, and we drove directly here. We saw some of the city coming in from the airport, but we look forward to seeing more."

Jenny noticed Phil's resemblance to his parents. Charles was tall and angular with black hair like Phil's. His features were sharp like Phil's but somewhat larger. Grace looked lovely in a pale yellow, linen dress that gracefully fitted her small-boned figure. She had a small, softly rounded face and black hair with a streak of gray. Her most striking feature—expressive, dark brown eyes—were exactly like Phil's.

After a pleasant conversation, the Harmons insisted that both Mary and Jenny go to dinner with them, but Mary was expecting a friend. After they said their goodbyes to Mary, Phil led them to his car. He put Jenny in the front seat beside him and drove to a seafood restaurant on the edge of town.

Seated around a window table overlooking a lake, the four happily laughed and talked together. Jenny could not help comparing Grace and Charles's open friendliness with Grant's more reserved parents. She asked polite questions and found, to her delight, that Dr. Harmon was doing medical research at a non-profit laboratory, having left his practice some years before.

"He loves his work, Jenny," Grace Harmon said, smiling at Jenny, "but I finally got him to take this time off. We are so proud of Phil. You know, his friend Chuck telephoned us and insisted that we stay with him."

Charles laughed good-naturedly. "Chuck's like the orientals, he makes us feel that we are honoring his house by staying there."

"But we're the ones who will feel honored," Grace said, "that he would have us there during his busy wedding preparations."

"How long can you stay?" Jenny asked.

"Chuck wants us to attend the wedding, so we'll leave after the wedding next Saturday," Charles said. "It seems that Chuck's parents are dead." Charles's face grew serious. "He has been like a brother to Phil, so we are adopting him."

All during this conversation, Jenny noticed that Phil sat serenely listening. She began to understand why he was so free of moodiness. He was the only child of these delightfully well-adjusted people. They had a joy in living that the Iversons could envy.

Grace turned to Jenny. "I understand that you'll be Evie's maid of honor."

"Yes, I'm looking forward to that."

Charles asked Phil about his practice, and thus began a long discussion about practicing medicine that lasted throughout the dinner, except when Grace would interrupt. But, on the whole, Grace seemed pleased to see the companionship that her husband and son were enjoying.

Fully satisfied with a delicious meal and good conversation, they walked out into the late June evening; the sun was setting and there was a cool breeze. "This is a beautiful part of the country," Charles said.

Phil drove them around the lake to see the large homes, then through the business district, and to the new medical offices on the edge of the city. Unlocking the door to the building, he gave them a tour. Charles, especially, was fascinated—he wanted to see each examining room, and he marveled at the complete laboratory, the towering shelves full of medical records, and the x-ray room. "You can do about everything here!" he exclaimed.

"Except surgery," Phil said.

As they walked out into the balmy June night, the scent of honeysuckle wafted toward them from the vines in the surrounding woods. "What a charming place," Grace said, as she stepped out onto the entrance walk.

"Son, you and Chuck are really set up well," Charles said. "It makes me homesick for my old practice. But I didn't have such a large operation."

"But you handled about as many patients," Phil said with discernible pride in his father.

"That's certain," Grace chimed in. "He worked too hard. Charles has looked and felt better since he quit his practice. He doesn't have hospital calls, but he still works long hours and often goes in Saturdays."

"I love my work," Charles said smiling and looking straight ahead, and every part of him proclaimed his sincerity.

They took Jenny home; and, as she left the car, she said, "I've really enjoyed being with all of you tonight." And she meant it.

"We must do this again," Charles said, as if the matter were settled.

"But next time, maybe Mary can come with us," Grace said. "Good night, Jenny. You are as beautiful as Phil said." Phil looked embarrassed.

Phil walked Jenny to the door. Alone together for a moment, they both felt a deeper bond for having had the richness of a family evening. It was dark; and, in the shadows, Phil and Jenny lingered in a kiss, a precious private moment, until Jenny handed Phil the door key. Phil turned the lock reluctantly and said, "I'll see you tomorrow, Jenny."

For the moment, she had forgotten that she was to go with all of them to Evie's for brunch and later to church the next morning. "I'll be ready at nine."

* * *

Chuck was waiting for them, when Phil and his parents returned. "Grace, Charles, I'm delighted to have you. Sorry I was at the hospital when you arrived."

They all shook hands and Charles said, "Congratulations on your coming marriage."

"Thank you," Chuck beamed. "I want you to sit on the right side at the wedding and on the front row as my family for the occasion."

"We would be honored, Chuck." Grace smiled at him.

Chuck slapped Phil on the back and said, "Your son here is

turning out to be a fine physician. He came in with me just as we completed our new offices."

"I took them over there tonight," Phil said.

"That is one more marvelous suite of offices," Charles said.

"And we toured the city—it's very beautiful," Grace added.

"June is one of our best months." Chuck got up. "Let me show you your room." He led them to a corner bedroom, where he had placed their bags on luggage racks and pointed out the adjoining bathroom. Back in the living room, Chuck served iced tea. "Evie is eager to meet you, but she had to stay home with the children tonight."

Phil leaned forward in his seat, rested his elbows on his knees, and turned to Charles and Grace. "Evie has two precious little children—Sally, five, and Josh, three."

Grace was delighted. "We want to see them."

"The children will be in the wedding," Chuck said, "but you'll see them when we go to Evie's tomorrow. I'm a lucky man—to get a beautiful woman and her children."

Charles leaned back and sipped his iced tea. "Nothing like being a parent, Chuck. You have a lot to look forward to."

"It's work, Chuck," Grace said, "but nothing is more fulfilling."

Chuck was smiling. "I will welcome parenthood."

* * *

On Sunday morning, Jenny awoke full of the memories of her day with Phil and his parents. She dressed in a beige silk skirt and blouse; and, just as she slipped on beige mid-heeled sandals, she heard Phil at the door and rushed downstairs to let him in.

"Hello, Jenny," he said smiling and his arms were wide open. Jenny slipped into them quickly, enjoying his embrace. He released her, took hold of her shoulders, and looked into her eyes. "My parents loved you."

* * *

On Sunday morning, Evie greeted Chuck, Grace, and Charles warmly. "Charles, Grace, these are my children, Sally and Josh." Charles couldn't resist leaning over and lifting Sally in the air. He put her down; then, holding Josh in his arms, he turned to Chuck. "I see what you mean, Chuck, you are getting some beautiful children."

Chuck, standing next to Evie, put his arm around her. "And," he said, "the beautiful mother!"

When Phil arrived with Jenny, they sat down to breakfast. "We'll need both cars for church," Chuck said, knowing they would take the children.

At church, they put the children in the nursery and, entering the crowded sanctuary, could not find seats together. Chuck and Evie went down the aisle to a seat near the front, so that the others could have the four seats near the back.

Phil, sharing a hymn book with Jenny, felt very happy and fulfilled to have his parents on one side and his beautiful Jenny on the other; and, during the sermon, he reflected on how far he had come spiritually since he had started praying with Chuck every morning in the hospital chapel.

Then, turning to smile at Jenny briefly, he realized how much he had changed since knowing her—her faith was contagious. If she had hinted that his spiritual life was less than it should be, he would have been offended; but, she had not taken a high ground position of being more spiritual. Instead, she had touched him through her compassion and her constant striving to affirm and comfort others. With his scientific training and keen mind, he liked to be reached through the mind. But he had been drawn into a deeper commitment to Christ by both Jenny's and Chuck's warm human relationships. Whatever it was that Jenny had, he wanted to have it; and he wanted her presence always.

During the sermon, Jenny sat quietly next to Phil; and, as they rose for the final hymn, she enjoyed feeling his towering presence beside her.

CHAPTER FIFTEEN

The sun was shining and it was a perfect June day. For Evie and Chuck's outdoor wedding, folding chairs had been set in rows in Chuck's backyard. Beyond, at the far end of the garden, a flower-laced arbor served as an altar.

Chuck and Phil took their places near the altar facing the aisle. As a string quartet played Mendelssohn's Wedding March, Sally, in a frilly dress with flowers in her hair, came down the grassy aisle, dropping rose petals in the path of the bride. Suddenly Josh, who was sitting with Mary, called out to Sally, causing everyone to laugh.

When Jenny came down the aisle in a long, pink silk dress carrying a bouquet of white roses, Phil was watching her every move; until, aware of his role as best man, he shifted his gaze to Evie's entrance in a long, pale silk dress, a shade lighter than Jenny's. As Evie joined Chuck and faced the altar, Jenny and Phil assumed their positions on each side.

Phil looked at Jenny standing across from him. She was altogether beautiful and desirable, and his dream of standing at an altar with her one day seemed closer. But he had been disturbed. Just before the rehearsal dinner, Evie had mentioned that Grant continued to call and that Jenny now had ambivalent feelings toward Grant. The comment had dampened his happiness at the rehearsal the night before and throughout the party later. Maybe Jenny still loved Grant; and, if she did, Phil was torn between fighting to win her and waiting to let her make a decision. He was not one to give up; but, to be fair, he would give her more time.

Jenny looked at Phil standing next to Chuck at the altar. He was very handsome in his black suit. His rich black hair fell forward somewhat on his forehead and framed his piercing yet richly warm brown eyes. But did he really care for her? Last night at the rehearsal dinner, he had seemed aloof. Sitting next to her at table, he had talked but he did not smile; and that hint of tenderness, which she had come to love, was not in his voice. She didn't understand the subtle change.

As Chuck stood beside Evie at the altar, he felt overwhelmed by his love for her. He felt that the deep love he had had for Laura, coupled with his several years of grief and loneliness, had come together in an even larger love for Evie. *And*, he thought, *she is so beautiful. To think that she will be mine.* Finding Evie had been a great blessing—her sense of peace, her quick intelligence, her efficient managing of her life had all impressed him. He was touched by her gift of mothering her children; and, while he had been inhibited by it in the past, he admired the way she had been loyal to Dan. *A woman such as this is a rarity*, he thought.

The minister was still talking as Evie and Chuck approached the point of taking their vows. Evie knew that her years of loneliness were gone. She loved Chuck as she had loved Dan, but how wonderful to have that love returned. Toward the end of Dan's life, she had felt that she was loving him in a vacuum—her emotions had not changed, but Dan's emotions were turned to Connie. For Evie, it had been like living a fantasy; yet, she had been unable to divest herself of a loyalty to him. She had longed to be loved; and now she would have Chuck, this kind and affectionate man as her husband, day in and day out, for the rest of their lives. Her heart was filled with thanksgiving.

When Chuck's minister pronounced them man and wife, Chuck kissed Evie, and the joyous wedding party walked back across the grassy aisle to Chuck's patio for the photographs and the reception. As they reached the patio, Evie threw her bouquet and Jenny caught it. Phil, who had been watching nearby, moved quickly to her side and hoped she like the idea of being the next bride.

After the garden reception, the newlyweds went into the house to change to traveling clothes. When they came out, Jenny, Phil, and the Harmons surrounded them. Mary stood nearby with both of the children.

"Be good to Mary," Evie admonished as she kissed each child, and Chuck swept them into his arms. Then they hugged everyone nearby, ran to the car, and, with the guests waving, sped away.

Charles Harmon turned to Phil and Jenny, "We'll have to be going, too."

"I wish you could stay longer," Jenny said. She really liked them.

"Thank you," Grace said, "I wish we could."

"I know Dad needs to get back to his lab," Phil said, knowing his dad's eagerness to get on the road.

"The car is loaded," Charles said. "Thank you, Mary and Jenny, for your hospitality. We'll call Chuck and thank him when he is less occupied."

Phil walked his parents to the car.

Grace turned to Phil, "Jenny is such a lovely girl, Phil. I truly enjoyed getting to know her."

"I'm glad," he said. "She's the person I hope to marry."

"I couldn't be happier," Grace said.

"Son," Charles said, slipping behind the wheel, "have you asked her yet?"

"Not yet. Jenny has been very hurt by someone in the past, and I am trying to move slowly and carefully." As soon as he said it, he knew it sounded like an excuse.

"Just don't move too slowly and let her get away—she's a keeper," Charles said.

* * *

During the next two weeks, while Chuck and Evie were on their honeymoon, Phil rarely saw Jenny. He was covering Chuck's patients with the help of another physician who was on call for him every other week. He missed Evie's quick assistance. He struggled on with a new substitute nurse; and, each day, he continued to see patients until early evening. He still prayed in the hospital chapel each morning for each of his patients, and he prayed for Jenny. He felt that he was getting an answer about Jenny—it was time for him to tell her how much he loved her. He called her now and then and hoped she understood that he had no free time just now.

* * *

Phil was overjoyed when the Carlsons returned from their trip. They moved the children and their furniture and toys into Chuck's house; and, as far as Phil could tell, the new family melded together beautifully in their new home. Chuck and Evie invited Phil and Jenny for dinner every week; and, one night, as Phil took Jenny home, he walked her to the door, took her face in his hands, and said, "Jenny, I love you very much. I hope that you have some feeling for me."

"I do, Phil. I feel that I'm falling in love with you."

"You aren't sure? Is Grant still calling?"

"Yes. He stirs up all sorts of emotions in me but now mostly negative ones."

"I love you enough to wait. I want you to find how you really feel."

As Jenny looked up and saw the love in Phil's eyes, she felt him pull her close and felt the sweetness of his kiss.

* * *

It was in late July, when Jenny, working at her desk, received the long-awaited phone call.

"Chaplain Carter?" a lady's voice came over the line."I'm calling from Paul Sherrill's office about your hearing with the Patients' Advocacy Committee."

A heavy dread filled Jenny's mind.

"We've set an appointment for August 15, at nine thirty. You can bring any documentation you wish."

"What sort of documentation?" Jenny said, feeling that she sounded stupid.

"Anything to support your defense," the pleasant female voice answered. "You can also bring any staff members who may corroborate your position."

"Thank you, I'll be there," Jenny answered. She put down the telephone at her desk and waited for Tom to return to the office.

The door to the reception room banged and she looked up to see Tom coming in, wearing a wet raincoat.

"A messy day," Tom said, as he placed a dripping umbrella against the wall. "Summer storms in this part of the country are so sudden—it's the mountain range nearby—affects the air currents."

"Tom, I need to talk to you."

"OK, shoot." He took off the plastic raincoat.

"My hearing has been set for August 15." Jenny saw the sudden contortion in his face.

"What?" he said loudly and flatly.

Had Tom talked to Paul again since he returned from his month off? Jenny knew that Tom was effective at everything he did and that his gruff, genial manner, not typical of chaplains, was pleasing to everyone. But, she also knew that he had made too many promises to too many people. He would not keep a planner or note pad; but, in his manly pride, relied on his memory.

Tom was speaking and answering the question in her mind. "I haven't talked to Paul again; but, now that it's referred to the full committee, I don't think there's anything we can do. What else did they say?"

"They said that I could bring documentation or any staff member to corroborate my case."

"What is this—a murder trial? Of all the silly nonsense. Jenny, I have to go see a family down near the operating room—the patient is in emergency surgery right now, but I'll go to before the

Patients' Advocacy Committee when the hearing comes up, so don't worry."

As usual, Tom was optimistic. Still, Jenny asked, "Have you heard of anyone being fired after these hearings?"

"Well, yes—there have been a few cases." Tom picked up his beeper. "But those people that were fired—that was different. Those were serious charges and this case is trivial." He started toward the door.

"Have you ever been reported to this committee?" she asked.

Tom pause at the door, looked at her for a moment and said, "No." Then he was gone.

Jenny sat still at her desk awhile—disappointed at the turn of events. She arose slowly and walked into the hospital chapel, the place where so many families had come with hearts totally broken and strained beyond what they felt they could endure. Kneeling in the darkened atmosphere, she prayed about the Gosnell hearing, committing the machinations of the hearing to God and seeking peace to face whatever lay ahead for her.

Then her mind moved to Phil as it often did these days. She felt in her spirit that God, in His wisdom, had sent this kind and happy man, whose spirituality blended with hers. She looked back on her engagement to Grant. There had never been the feeling of wholeness that she experienced with Phil. She prayed that God would lift all the strange and unpleasant feelings she had about Grant so that she could be free to love Phil. Then, she arose and left the chapel in peace.

CHAPTER SIXTEEN

Mary Carter was ready to leave the house, when the phone rang. Probably for Jenny, she thought.

"Mrs. Carter, this is Norma Iverson. I was in the area and I wanted to meet you."

"Well, Norma," Mary was surprised. What could she say? "I'd love to have you come on out to see me. We live in North Morristown."

"I know. I have directions."

"I'll be expecting you."

Soon a cream-colored Lincoln pulled into Mary's driveway. Mary opened the door to see a tall, elegant lady, beautifully dressed and beautifully coiffed.

"Mary?" she said.

"Norma, come in." Mary led her to a chair in the living room and offered coffee.

"No, thank you anyway. I can't stay long; and, of course, Grant doesn't know I'm here."

"Really?" Mary, trying to be courteous, asked, "How is Grant?"

"As well as can be expected. You know," Norma said with great dramatic emphasis, "Mr. Iverson and I have separated."

"Yes, I believe Jenny told me."

"And it hasn't been easy, but I've enjoyed having Grant back home. You know Bob Harrington has promoted Grant to Regional Manager now."

It was obvious that Norma was proud. Mary tried to think of something exemplary to say about Grant, but her emotions got in the way. All she could say was a mere statement of fact, "I know you're proud of him."

"He's always been an achiever. He's very smart."

"I'm sure he is." Mary's patience was growing thin.

"But as successful as he is, he still misses Jenny."

"Well, I'm glad to say that Jenny finally seems to be happy again. Grant's canceling the wedding so suddenly hurt her very much, but she has come a long way since then." Not once, Mary noted, had Norma asked how Jenny was.

"I wanted you to understand, Mary, that Mr. Iverson and I separated once before when Grant was a little boy. It disturbed him dreadfully. It was he and I against the world. Since Mr. Iverson moved out this winter, Grant and I have become bonded again as we were then."

"But Grant will want to marry some day," Mary said, closely watching Norma's face. "If not to Jenny, to someone else."

"Oh, I know. And I thought it was all set. He has been dating Bob Harrington's daughter, Marilyn, who is very involved in community activities. She and I became very close, and I had hoped they would marry. I know that Marilyn wanted that. But right at the last, Grant dashed our hopes by saying he was still in love with Jenny."

"You don't say." Mary's tone was icy.

"That's why I came. I thought that you might encourage Jenny to give Grant another chance."

"You'd need to talk to Jenny about that. I try not to interfere in her life to that extent."

"But Grant tells me that he has trouble even getting in touch with Jenny " Her tone was disparaging. "He really wants to talk to her, and she doesn't return his calls."

Mary's heart rate shot up. "Look, Norma!" her voice was stern. "You and I cannot broker a relationship between Grant and Jenny. And, after his behavior, I'm not sure that I would want to try."

"But please try. You never know when a well placed word from you will have an effect."

"Norma," Mary said in exasperation, "why don't you let Grant go. Let him fight his own battles and take the consequences for his actions."

"But I love him so. He's such a comfort to me. I'd prefer things to go on as they are, of course; but, if Jenny is what he really wants, I want to help him win her again. You know, my heart flutters sometimes. My doctor thinks it is caused by anxiety, but I know that there is really something wrong with my heart."

"I believe there is," Mary said as her mouth tightened.

Norma slowly rose from her chair. "Well, I must be going. I'm sorry that you can't see your way clear to help us."

"I don't have that power." Mary walked with her to the door. "And, Norma, let me recommend that you build a life for yourself and let Grant work out his own problems. I've been where you are, a woman alone. My husband died two years ago, and I have tried not to make Jenny fill my unmet needs. Jenny lives at home because she chooses to. We have a friendship, but I have my own friends and activities. I understand that you have your civic activities to keep you involved."

"I did before the divorce." Her mouth tightened. "Thank you, Mary, for your hospitality." Norma turned and walked to her car.

Mary closed the door, walked into the living room, sighed and sat down. *Poor Grant. Poor Jenny. Thank you, Lord, that Jenny did not marry into that family.*

* * *

When Jenny came home from the hospital that night, Mary told her of Norma's visit.

"I can't believe that Mrs. Iverson would try to intervene," Jenny said in unbelief. She sat down and thought a minute. "But, I guess she loves him so."

Mary could not restrain herself. "Jenny, Norma's love is self-serving. She is controlling too. I hope she will let him go." Looking at Jenny's innocent expression, Mary realized that Jenny was unwilling to see Norma's self-centeredness.

Jenny, still sitting, looked out the living room window as if she were trying to gather her thoughts. "Did she mention that she had wanted Grant to marry Bob Harrington's daughter?"

Mary looked surprised. "Well, yes."

"Grant told me that, the first time he was here. He seemed to think I would admire him for resisting both Marilyn and his mother."

"Well, you'll have to give him that. He did stand up to a very resolute mother. But Jenny," she took her hand, "I'm glad that you are sensible about all this."

Jenny sighed. "I may as well be. I came to accept Grant's change of heart long ago. His earnestness now really doesn't please me. I am happy at last, and I don't want that to change."

* * *

On the day of the hearing, Jenny and Tom took the elevator to the conference room. As they entered, she was relieved to see that Paul Sherrill and five committee members were there, but Glenn Warren was not. Paul, a tall, imposing figure with thick white hair, sat at the end of a long, highly polished conference table. He rose, shook their hands, and greeted them warmly. As they took their seats at the table, Jenny noticed that Barry McMillan, sitting at the other end of the table, again avoided eye contact with her.

Paul opened the meeting. "Jenny, we have the report of Glenn Warren's preliminary meeting with you. He believes that the patient, Elizabeth Gosnell, felt pressured by you to pray. Will you elaborate on that?"

"As I told Glenn Warren, I visited Mrs. Gosnell and asked about her surgery. After a time, I asked if she would like a prayer."

"Then you did ask her permission?"

"Yes, of course. When I found that she did not want prayer, I changed the subject, but I did stay for some time to visit."

Paul looked at the file. "So, you believe that she felt no pressure in any way."

"That's correct."

"Did you visit her again?"

"Yes, I visited her once more and we had a chat."

"Did you offer to pray that time?"

"No, I always honor the patient's wishes."

Tom signaled to Paul, "May I ask a question?"

"Of course." Paul turned toward Tom.

"Has there ever been a written complaint from Mrs. Gosnell about Jenny?"

"No, and that's part of our problem here." Paul said. "We normally handle complaints from patients or from their families. It's unusual to receive the complaint from an employee. But, since Barry, here," he looked at Barry, "feels strongly about this and has himself filled out a complaint, we are obligated to look into it."

Jenny was silent.

Paul looked at the committee members and asked if they had questions.

One person, a nurse, spoke, "I believe Jenny. She comes into our Neurotrauma unit and is very careful in how she approaches the patients. In fact, she has prayed with us—that is, when we asked her to."

"Any other comments or questions?"

The Committee members were unusually quiet. They sat looking at Jenny and it was hard for her to read their thoughts.

Paul continued, "Our committee has reviewed Glenn's preliminary report; and we have decided that, in order to consider this case, we must contact the patient. After all, it's her rights that we are entrusted to protect." Paul paused and looked at Jenny, then at Tom.

"So Jenny, Tom, we have asked the hospital attorney to contact Mrs. Gosnell and give her an opportunity to file a complaint if she wishes. The attorney will also determine if there is a possibility of a lawsuit. We don't think there is, but we are taking this precaution."

Tom spoke up, "So when will this be resolved?"

"We hope within a week—two weeks at the most."

Silence.

"Well, Jenny, do you have any questions? Paul asked.

"No, I guess not."

"Well, that completes our work with you Jenny; we'll go on to our next case. Thank you for coming."

* * *

Once Tom and Jenny were outside the conference room, Tom said, "See, there was nothing to it."

"Yes, I'm glad it's over with. I was surprised that Barry was quiet."

"I think they're on to him." Tom said, "Jenny, you're not on duty today so go home and try to forget all this. We'll get the final dismissal soon, I know."

Thanking Tom, she left the hospital.

CHAPTER SEVENTEEN

Two weeks later, Jenny was relieved when Paul Sherrill called to say that the case had been dismissed. "Our attorney contacted Mrs. Gosnell," he said, "and found that she had no grievance. She insisted that she did not want to file a complaint. She could barely remember her remark to Barry McMillan."

Tom walked in the door. "Thank you, Paul. Tom is here, can you hold?"

Tom grabbed his phone, "Paul, is it over?"

"Yes, and I was about to tell Jenny that the committee voted against noting the complaint on her employment record."

"Now you're talking. You know, Jenny's very careful. She would never do anything to cause a complaint."

"I think we know that. And, Jenny, my concern is that this experience would make you timid with the patients. I hope you'll continue to use the freedom you've had in your work. This has been a strange complaint, seeing that your job description includes praying with the patients. I think Barry was off base to blow up this incident."

"I don't have any hard feelings toward Barry, Paul. He's working from his own belief system."

"Well, I think he'll be quiet for awhile," Paul said.

Tom said, "Paul, we appreciate all you did to help Jenny."

"Well, I didn't do anything—the committee was all for dismissing the complaint. You know, Tom, I worked with the Director when he wanted to establish the chaplain program, and we all consider it a source of pride."

That comment caused Tom to smile. He put down the phone,

turned to Jenny, and said, "I'm glad it turned out all right. Jenny, we prayed and we know that He never fails us."

"I know," Jenny said, humbled. "Thank you, Tom, for your support." Now that it was over, she longed to tell the news to Phil, but he would be with his patients now. She would have to wait until he came over to her house tonight.

* * *

That night, as Jenny dressed for her date with Phil, her heart was light; and she felt divinely happy. With the problem at work solved, she could relax and dream of all the possibilities that lie ahead. She was sure that Phil loved her and more sure every day of her love for him. When the phone rang, she hoped that Phil had not been detained with a patient.

"Jenny?" It was Grant. "I'm in town for a few hours and I wanted to stop by to see you."

"This isn't a good time, Grant. I have a date tonight."

"I won't stay long. I just want to see you a minute."

"Can't we discuss it on the phone?"

"No, I'm coming over. I'll see you in a few minutes." Then he hung up the phone.

Jenny looked at the clock—it was half past six and Phil was coming at seven. Whatever it was Grant had to say, he had better say it quickly. She finished dressing quickly and headed down the steps just as the doorbell rang. Mary was in the living room and Jenny called to her. "That's Grant at the door—he said he wouldn't stay long—Phil is coming at seven."

Mary called, "Good luck!"

Jenny opened the door and led Grant onto the patio. "Grant, what on earth? What is it that can't wait?"

"I can't wait Jenny," he said, taking her hand.

She pulled her hand away and sat down. His face looked tired—like that night nine months ago when she sat across from him at Mario's.

"Jenny, I've been calling you since June, and you've refused to go out with me."

She looked hard at him. "Grant when you broke our engagement, I didn't understand why. But I had to accept it. Why can't you accept it now when I say that I'm interested in someone else?"

"But you're not engaged yet, are you?"

"No. Grant, I've wanted to be kind—I've tried to avoid a confrontation. But you keep popping up at the wrong time—like tonight. And even your mother pops up." She regretted saying that.

"Uh—Mother? Well, yeah, she told me about that, but she was just trying to help. Jenny," he said, "I'm asking you to forget the past—I know I can make you happy."

"If we had remained friends," Jenny said softly, "there might have been a chance." She thought that he had been cruel to disappear and to stop all contact. All along, she had believed that, if they had remained friends, she would not have felt so deserted and humiliated. Now, she realized that she could not have been just friends with Grant.

"Mother has given me some property where we could build a house, and I don't have to travel anymore," he was saying. "And, now, even my mother wants me to marry you."

Jenny stared at him. "She didn't before?"

"Well, you know Mother." He avoided eye contact.

"Really!" her voice had an edge to it.

"But now she sees that I'm unhappy without you."

Jenny was determined to remain calm. She looked at her watch, then stood up abruptly. "My friend will be here soon."

Grant kept talking and followed her as she walked out onto the grass and toward the sidewalk where his car was parked. He lingered until she started to move away; then finally got into his car. He drove away only when he saw Phil's car pull up behind him.

Jenny stood on the sidewalk in the late day sun and smiled at Phil as he came toward her. She felt that everything was resolved and that she was free at last. Phil embraced her. "You look beautiful, Jenny," he said.

At that moment, he looked beautiful to her. "You do, too." she laughed.

Holding hands, they strolled into the house. "Let me get my purse," Jenny said, letting him in the door. They said good night to Mary, who was reading in the living room, and went back into the hall, where Jenny picked up her purse. "I'm ready," she said, and there was laughter in her voice.

Phil responded with a smile, but his voice was tense. "That was Grant who just pulled away, wasn't it?"

"Yes, and he won't be back."

Phil looked into Jenny's eyes with deep concern. "Are you sure?"

"Very sure!" she said, and reached up to embrace him.

He swept her up into his arms and whispered, "Oh, Jenny, I love you so much."

As they went out the door, Mary looked up from her book. She could not avoid hearing the exchange. She didn't know what had happened with Grant, but she was glad that Phil had won. She went to the window and watched with delight as the happy pair got into Phil's car and drove off. As she turned around, she caught her image in a mirror—*mother of the bride*, she thought. She hadn't decided what she would wear, but she stood erect and envisioned how she would look at the wedding.

* * *

Jenny and Phil had their wedding in Jenny's church, with family and friends gathered. Mary had decided what to wear; and, when she walked to her seat on the arm of an usher, she felt beautiful in her beige, lace, street-length dress.

"Mary, you'll be next in this wedding marathon," Chuck had said just before the wedding; but, as Mary sat in her seat on the front row, she was totally content with her memories of Howard and content with Jenny, the visible and beautiful outcome of their love. Feeling a rush of love for her daughter and her new son-in-law, she dabbed her eyes with a handkerchief.

Grace and Charles Harmon sat on the front row of the groom's side of the church, happy to be called back to Morristown so soon and for this reason. Filled with pride about Phil, they now felt that they had found the daughter they had always wanted.

Phil and Chuck walked out together to face the congregation. Phil was nervous but smiling. Chuck, standing quietly next to his friend, could barely contain his joy. They both smiled as they saw little Sally again making a trip down the aisle in her frilly outfit, dropping roses in the bride's path.

Evie entered and walked down the aisle in the same pale pink, silk dress she had worn in her wedding. Radiant from her own new-found happiness, she was thrilled that Jenny would soon be coming down the aisle behind her to marry Phil.

Finally, Jenny came down the aisle alone. She had not wanted anyone to substitute for her beloved dad. Her sleeveless, white satin wedding dress had a round neckline, and its full embroidered skirt fell into a train. A mist of white tulle veiling attached to a flowered tiara fell along the train of her dress.

Phil broke into a wide smile as he watched her approach. When it was time for them to take their vows, they turned to face each other. As Phil took Jenny's white-gloved hands into his and looked into her glowing eyes, he could see just a few strands of her auburn hair surrounded by the full white veil. The minister read his vows; and Phil, enchanted as he looked at Jenny, did not hear his cue. The soft laughter that rippled throughout the congregation brought him to attention, and he repeated the vow.

As Jenny looked into Phil's eyes and repeated her vows, she knew that she was exactly where God would have her.

And Phil, in his heart, dedicated his all—for the love of Jenny.

Printed in the United States
2394